Margaret Elizabeth Munson Sangster

Cheerful To-ays and Trustful To-morrows

Vol. 1

Margaret Elizabeth Munson Sangster

Cheerful To-ays and Trustful To-morrows
Vol. 1

ISBN/EAN: 9783337375447

Printed in Europe, USA, Canada, Australia, Japan

Cover: Foto ©Andreas Hilbeck / pixelio.de

More available books at **www.hansebooks.com**

CHEERFUL TO-DAYS

AND

TRUSTFUL TO-MORROWS

BY

MARGARET E. SANGSTER

Author of " Life on High Levels," "Maidie's Problem,"
" Home Life Made Beautiful," Etc.

———————

"As thy days, so shall thy strength be."
"Underneath are the everlasting arms."

NEW YORK

EATON & MAINS

TO

My Brother John

WHO, WITH ME, REMEMBERS REVERENTLY

OUR

Father and Mother

CONTENTS

CONTENTS

LIST OF ILLUSTRATIONS

CHEERFUL TO-DAYS
AND
TRUSTFUL TO-MORROWS

CHAPTER I

FREEDOM FROM WORRY

SHE was not young and her path had been
rough and steep, this dear little mother whose
sweet face shines upon me, out of the dim past,
like a beautiful beaming star. It was a face
which kept to old age something of its childish
sweetness and eagerness of expression, for to
this dear one it was given never to lose the child
heart, and it was, and is, unto such as she that
our blessed Lord has always revealed the inner
meaning of the Kingdom. Wistful and loving
and animated, let cares and burdens be ever so
numerous, it was hers to know the full blessedness of that text, "The beloved of the Lord
shall dwell in safety by him." Her sorrows had
been many. She had known the exquisite pain

of losing her firstborn in his lovely babyhood, she had seen an older laddie stricken down in a moment, and through one never forgotten summer she had watched the gradual decline of another precious son; so that three times the light had been blotted from her sky and the noonday had been as the night.

Then, from wonderful and elastic health, she had been plunged into the long weariness of an invalid's life. It began with a serious illness which followed closely upon her widowhood, while her three remaining children were all very young. That exhausting illness, in which for weeks she hung upon the border land and which brought her to the very edge of the dark river, so that life seemed to pull her out and back when her feet were cold in the rushing flood, and her family, her pastor and her physician had all given her up, left her at last, but with only the fragments of the strong constitution she had once had. The twenty-five remaining years were more or less a battle, and she fought that battle with a persistent courage and a quality of cheerfulness which she could never have had if One like unto the Son of God had not been ever at her side.

She had been tried also in the crucible of limited means. The house must be kept, the children must be educated, the Lord's tenth must be devoted, and the purse was always narrow, and sometimes the gray gaunt wolf not only scratched at the door but dared to put his head inside. Never mind. He was always thrust back, and the door slammed boldly in his face. Kith and kin of hers were few but those she had stood by her in loyalty of love and trust, and hers was the spirit of one, her friend, who in similar circumstances said, "I have no fear. If it be necessary for the Lord to work a miracle for my children and me he will do it."

The barrel of meal did not waste, and the cruse of oil did not fail, though now and then the scoop was scanty and there were but few drops in the flask. The children grew up, there were books around them, they were sent to the best schools; their advantages were not lessened because their earthly father had left them no fortune except a sunny temperament and a boundless trust in God.

One great advantage they had, that it never even occurred to them to complain of their lot, to regard self-denial as a hardship, or to apolo-

gize for anything in their surroundings. One
day a second-hand piano came home. Their
little parlor, with its ingrain carpet, marble-
topped table and six haircloth-covered chairs,
appeared to them a drawing room fit for a queen
—as indeed it was, for a queen presided over it
and sat there smiling and happy when the little
daughter ran her fingers up and down the ivory
keys.

The grace of freedom from worry was always
in that home.

One evening, at the end of a rather tedious
day, when the money was low and the coal in
the bin was also low and winter was sounding
his advance in chill blasts of the north wind
and fierce tussles of the bare tree boughs, the
little mother went to her room for a half hour's
rest. She always said that she was lying wide
awake, that she had not so much as fallen asleep
for an instant, and if we thought that she was
mistaken we never told her so; for, whether it
was a dream or whether it was a vision, the Lord
of glory vouchsafed a comforting revelation of
himself by means of it to the handmaid whose
chief joy was his service.

She said she was aware suddenly of a presence in the room. "I looked about," here her blue eyes grew very soft and earnest, "to see if it was M. or Isa, but I had not heard the door open, and the door was shut. Nobody was there. But all above and around me the atmosphere grew bright, and through the clear brightness formed a something still more radiant and golden, bending and brooding over me as I lay in the bed and looked up, and then, sweet and very tender, came a word I heard in my heart just as if a voice had spoken:

"'My God shall supply all your need. Be not faithless, but believing.'"

Dream or vision, it gave her new strength for the way and she arose and went on, rejoicing in the Lord.

We hear a good deal in these days about the futility of worry, and there are many who try to live in the peace and serenity which come from abandoning all needless anxiety. But I cannot quite understand how any of us, in this peculiarly changeful world, can live in entire freedom from this scourge unless we follow the apostolic injunction, "In everything by prayer and supplication with thanksgiving let your requests be made known unto God."

It is the Christian's privilege to meet every situation with an undaunted front, never to be taken by surprise, never to be found off guard. While it is comparatively easy to cease from worry for one's self, we all know how hard it is not to carry vicarious worries. The son, dear as your own life, who loses his position and cannot find another, the daughter, a few years ago like a rose in bloom, so fresh, so fair, now crippled with rheumatism, or failing before your eyes with some relentless and subtle malady which defies medical skill, the husband stricken in his prime with paralysis, and thenceforward all his days compelled to walk softly, the friend bereaved, and unable to rise above the weight of grief, the acquaintance taking a wrong turn in the road, the pastor unappreciated in his parish, all the wonderful social network woven around our homes and affections —how difficult it is to refrain from worry about these.

For, you see, sympathy is as much a daily duty as tranquillity, and we are as really bound to fulfill the law of Christ by bearing one another's burdens as by cessation from the strain of fretting and fussing and fuming, of wearing ourselves and our friends out by unavailing care.

The secret of the blessedness which sets us free to serve is, I am sure, found only in unreserved acceptance of the will of God as best for us and ours, and in daily communion with the Master. Once we have lived into that dear and intimate friendship with Jesus which enables us to feel, without a question, that his will is not only his choice for us but ours too, we step into a land of serenity where never intrudes a single chilling blast of doubt.

"I know no life divided,
  O Lord of life, from thee."

"I would rather walk with God in the dark
Than walk alone in the light."

"Looking to Jesus—
  Ever serener,
Working or suffering,
  Be thy demeanor."

There is absolutely no possibility of worry for the soul which thus knows the Lord.

Of course there are differences of disposition which must be taken into account. Happy are they whom the Lord, from their cradles, has endowed with a capacity for discerning the sun behind the clouds. To see the bright side instinctively is a rare and gracious gift. A man of "cheerful yesterdays and confident to-morrows" is usually a pleasant companion, and a good comrade on the road of life. In Mrs. Oliphant's recently published autobiography—the story it is of a very brave and noble life—there is a chapter in which she tells how she had come to a crisis in her affairs, and there were a number of helpless people depending on her and her little slender pen.

"I recollect coming home in a kind of despair and being met at the door, when it was opened to me, by the murmur of the merry house, the cheerful voices, the overflowing home, every corner full and warm as if it had a steady income and secure revenue at its back. I used to work very late then, always till two in the morning; I can't remember whether I worked that night, but I think it was one of the darkest nights and I could not think what I should do."

Next morning came an unexpected visitor, and unexpected help, and "the road did run round that corner after all. Our Father in heaven had settled it all the time for the children; there had never been any doubt. I was absolutely without hope or help. I did not know where to turn, and here, in a moment, all was clear again—the road free in the sunshine, the cloud in a moment rolled away."

God's dear child ought not to have been without *hope*. There is always blue sky somewhere, and all things are always working together for good to those who love God. The peace that passeth all understanding shall keep us, as the sentry keeps the camp, if we but trust and obey.

CHAPTER II

REPOSE OF MANNER

EVEN if one is conscious of agitation and turmoil underneath, there is a distinct gain in its control by the cultivation of repose of manner. Largely this may be a matter of habit, and one may so discipline her muscles, and so accustom them to obedience, that she will repress the petulant frown, forbid her lips the down-drooping curve, and train her body to express ease and quiet rather than impatience and irritability. The dignity of a tranquil demeanor so far exceeds the opposite—lack of poise—which is shown in undue emphasis, in jerky movements, and frequent complaint, that for its mere beauty, aside from its ethical value, one should seek its possession. All the varieties of scolding, nagging, fault-finding, and bemoaning one's fate, born of insufficient self-respect and of intermittent self-control, are impossible to her who has made repose her garment of defense, her chain armor, against the world.

A good deal of our flurried and perturbed manner we owe to our tendency to indulge in both work and play beyond our strength. We do not know when to stop. We carry our golfing, our skating, our tennis, our driving, riding and walking to such an extent that instead of adding to our stock of health they exhaust it; and if this be true of recreation it is still more true of work. The mother is sewing on the little frock, and it must be finished by Saturday night. The frills and puffs and tucks are so elaborate that the sewing on the small maiden's Sabbath raiment is appalling if one remembers the drain that fine stitching makes on a not over-vigorous woman, so that she feels at last as if a sudden step on the floor or an unexpected question would make her scream or jump. Two questions arise: Why should a child's frock be other than simple? A plain little smock with no elaboration of ornament, with only a deep hem, is appropriate for any little girl, be her station what it may. The washerwoman's daughter and the queen's, during those happy years between three and twelve, should so far as style is concerned be dressed precisely alike. Then, why must the frock be done by a certain hour; why must there be a new frock always for Sunday's wearing? Few small maidens are without a change of clothing, and all that is requisite for church and Sunday school is something whole and clean, dainty from the laundry or the wardrobe, but not necessarily new. The mother would do far better for herself and her child by stopping her work before she is very tired, and by saving her nervous force for the pleasure of her home life.

Many a cross word is needlessly spoken, many a jarring chord is struck, many a time the wheels of the household grate harshly along the road, because there is friction in the mother's temper. The temper which is adjusted to the day, which is fine-edged and keen yet never morose, which meets every difficulty with a brave spirit and never prints itself on a clouded countenance, is worth having, worth striving for, worth praying for day by day. If we can gain repose nowhere else we can find it in the little sanctuary of the closet.

"I always knew when mother had been talking with God," said a man whose Christian life was full of sweetness and who was widely influential. "She had a little room at the end of the hall, and when she went in and shut fast the door we children walked softly past, for we knew that in there our mother was kneeling at the mercy seat." When she came forth her face shone.

Another and contrasting picture comes to my mind. "I never was intimate with my mother, nor anything but afraid of her until I was eighteen years old," said a lady, a shadow of pain on her face. "Before my birth mother had had a great grief and she turned away from God. Her looks were always severe, and she was cold to her children though I do think she loved them."

A woman who in middle life retains the freshness of girlhood in her complexion, and its grace in her step, whose face is the mirror of a beautiful soul, was one day asked how, during a long experience of physical suffering, she had kept herself from outward appearance of distress, from lines and marks which pain often leaves. "For one thing," she said, "I know my Heavenly Father appoints everything, and so I take with joy whatever he sends. Then I know, too, that every trace of impatience in thought must leave its finger print on my face, so I am careful never to look fretful even for a moment."

We have heard a great deal about the value of relaxation at certain intervals during our busiest days. Do we try it? If I could persuade you, whose eyes are tired out, to simply fold your hands and close your eyes for five minutes every hour I should soon convince you that the weariness would be greatly relieved. If, now and then, we who cannot take our hands from the domestic helm—from the cooking and pickling and preserving, and the management of the house—would go by ourselves, sit down in a rocking-chair or lie upon a lounge for fifteen minutes, allowing the mind to be a blank and the thoughts to fasten upon nothing, while hands and feet cease their clinging hold upon existence and relax as a baby's do, we should discover that there is magic in even these bits of rest between times. And if every busy house-mother would just lie down one hour in the middle of the day, or retire by herself one hour every afternoon and read or think or sleep as she chose, she would live longer and be happier for the experiment.

Said a wise physician to his wife, "My dear,

there is one thing on which I insist, and it is that you take the hour from three to four every afternoon and keep it for your own needs. Go to your own room and shut everybody out. I shall not intrude upon you; no one else shall be permitted to intrude upon you—friend, servant, or child. Be alone then, and do whatever you please, but never intermit your hour of entire freedom and rest." "To this kind provision for my health and comfort," said the wife, long afterward, "I am indebted for my elasticity of mind and body."

I am not sure how far the multiform public activities of to-day are responsible for the jaded looks and loss of repose visible in some of our friends. To belong to a woman's club, with its agreeable social opportunities, its reading and discussing of literary papers, and its frequent beneficent efforts beyond its doors, is, for many women, an excellent thing; broadening their horizon, and either enlarging their knowledge of current events or refreshing their memories of world movements in the past. But some women belong to three, five, or seven clubs simultaneously; others are taxed by an excessive amount of church work, a few undertaking and

carrying forward that which should be the task
of all. As repose of manner is hardly consistent with the mental state which knows the pressure of haste, and of too many conflicting engagements, it is not to be attained by her who
is bound by too strong a tether to boards, associations and clubs.

May I repeat for you a beautiful prayer, written by Rowland Williams?

"O God, who makest cheerfulness the companion of strength but apt to take wings in time
of sorrow, we humbly beseech thee if, in thy sovereign wisdom, thou sendest weakness yet for
thy mercy's sake deny us not the comfort of
patience. Lay not more upon us, O Heavenly
Father, than thou wilt enable us to bear; and,
since the fretfulness of our spirits is more hurt-
ful that the heaviness of our burden, grant us
that heavenly calmness which comes of owning
thy hand in all things, and patience in the trust
that thou doest all things well. Amen."

> "Wherever in the world I am,
>   In whatsoe'er estate,
> I have a fellowship with hearts
>   To keep and cultivate,
> A work of lowly love to do
>   For the Lord on whom I wait.

"I ask thee for the daily strength
  To none that ask denied,
A mind to blend with outward life
  While keeping at thy side;
Content to fill a little space
  If thou be glorified.

"There are briers besetting every path
  That call for patient care;
There is a cross in every lot,
  And need for earnest prayer;
But a lowly heart that leans on thee
  Is happy anywhere."

CHAPTER III

When the Children Are Around Us

I do not think life holds to any lips a sweeter cup, more honey-brimmed, more sparkling, than that the mother tastes when first she holds her little one in her arms. For this divine draught of pleasure she has dared the uttermost waves of anguish, has fought a duel with death, has plunged into depths of weakness and known mysterious perils which only motherhood understands. Yet every woman who has ever borne a babe will tell you that in the supreme hour of victory and joy she remembers the agony no more; it is blotted out by the flood of bliss beyond language or thought to describe. She and her child, bone of her bone, flesh of her flesh, these two—the new human being and the mother who cradled him under her arms before she held him in their tender circle—there is in all the world no bond like theirs; there is no glory of happiness which equals that which comes to any mother with any baby.

And yet we know of reluctant maternity, and we constantly see women refusing alike its penalties and its rewards, committing sin that they may evade it, declining to wear the most honorable of crowns and to assume the most potent of scepters. It is the peculiar loss of some women that they weigh in the balances the inconveniences and burdens of motherhood on the one hand, and its royal privileges on the other, and are afraid, or unwilling, or distrustful, and so rob themselves of their most beautiful right.

There are childless women to whom God has denied the boon of motherhood. When this is his will it is to be accepted without repining, and such women are often compassionate and comprehending toward the children of others; toward the orphan, or the sick, or the poor who need helpers. Wives there are who deliberately choose to have no babes. And this is not always from selfish motives, sometimes it is from those of a high and conscientious order of thought; they fear that they could not rightly guide little children. As the years pass, when old age arrives, the childless people are the lonely people, and they are apt to realize that they have lost some very precious things from life; some wealth which they might have had but which they have missed.

If one baby is a great delight then how much greater is a full nursery. When the brood is all under the mother's eye and hand at once the care may be incessant yet there is no end to the satisfaction. To see them all started for the day clean and well and dressed and wholesome and happy, to see them all tucked safe and cozy into their beds at night, each bairn with its prayers said and its story of the day told, what can be more thoroughly filled with the essence of homely content!

I am often very sorry for the first and for the only child, both being apt to receive an over share of discipline. Not invariably is it the good of the child which the mother seeks when she hedges its pathway with a bristling border of prickly "don'ts" and finds herself at her wit's end to devise original punishments. We are strangely complex, and even a loving mother may occasionally be vain and may reprove and rebuke her child rather because its mistakes wound her vanity than because she is honestly seeking the child's benefit.

"Tucked Safe and Cozy, into their Beds."

In child nurture perfect candor and confidence between mother and children are to be sought beyond every other thing. Spontaneity in a child is dwarfed by the entrance of fear into his heart, and whatever he does or says he should not be afraid to let mother see and hear it. Truth exercised toward a child, the keeping of one's word absolutely, the observance of one's promises, and truth maintained in the character, in the child's world there never being admitted a lie—that evil growth—will go far in preventing a child from falsity. Never ought we to doubt our little one's word. However extraordinary the statement made, however improbable, I prefer to accept it without hesitation if my child make it, remembering, as I do, that a child lives in a wonder world of fancy and that his vocabulary and mine are often different. To doubt a child when others are present is as great an offense as to give the lie to one who is grown up; greater, indeed, because the child is defenseless and forbidden to resent the outrage.

By every means in our power we should cultivate imagination in the little folk around us, for later on this gift of the skies will assist them in understanding God. A purely literal

mind has always more difficulty in attaining
to faith than one in which the ideal predomi-
nates. No sensible mother forgets that her little boy and girl play every day in fairyland, and
she does not prohibit them from hearing fairy
stories. They should hear the dear old favorites, "Cinderella," "Jack the Giant Killer,"
"Hop o' My Thumb," and all the rest, and on
the nursery shelf should stand the books of
Hans Andersen and the brothers Grimm, and
any other volumes of fairy lore which the
mother may approve. Alternate these with
Bible stories, so that Noah, Moses, David, Daniel, Ruth, Nehemiah and Esther may be familiar names to the child, and their lives a part
of his mental wealth, and you cannot go astray
in beginning their education. Long before a
child can read his mind should be well stored
with folk lore and Biblical learning. Poetry
comes next, and she is wise who recites to her
children songs and hymns and ballads worth
repeating, filled with the spirit of genuine verse,
while the memory most readily receives and
most strongly retains impressions.

Obedience is a corner stone of character building, and we cannot do without it when the chil-

dren are about us, not that we may enforce our own will but that they may learn the first principles of self-government. Just here some mothers and fathers blunder, insisting on blind subservience because they "say so" instead of building their own authority on that of the Lord. A little child is not a brute beast, and even brute beasts are better trained when their obedience is gained by unvarying gentleness, in accordance with the laws of the road, than when it is compelled by severity and apparent caprice. A dog trained by patient love is a charming comrade; subdued by arbitrary violence he is a cringing coward. Fortunately, few mothers in these enlightened days believe that a child's will should be broken, though here and there one finds a survivor of a more rigid period who expects to have an issue and a battle royal, or several of these, before the poor little one learns to bow to the fetich of implicit obedience.

For its own sake the family must have around it the safeguard of law. Within clearly defined law there is always liberty for the law-keeping. From the very beginning, by gentle inflexibility, the loving mother will direct the little feet into the straight path, and by her own example will show them how simple and sweet a thing is obedience. Whenever the rule of the home is obedience to the Heavenly Father the children will readily fall into docility towards the earthly parents.

Our children unconsciously reproduce our tones, our gestures, our ways of thinking and speaking. Imitation, voluntary or involuntary, crystallizes into habit, and habit decides our outward semblance to the world. Take the table, for instance. One's behavior at table shows the effect of good breeding almost unerringly. The gently bred person is considerate of others at the board, is familiar with the accepted etiquette of the knife, fork, and spoon, eats in moderation and silently, and automatically acknowledges every courtesy with an unobtrusive word of thanks. The boor violates every precept and tramples on our sense of the fitness of things; yet he may be a man of kind impulses and sterling integrity, unfortunate in having in early youth mingled with those who were ignorant of social usages. Constant and unvarying politeness exercised toward children, as well as exacted from them, will give them an ease and grace of bearing which will stand them

in stead when, in the future, they are no longer
under the safe shelter of the home roof.   Never
should a voice be raised in scolding or anger in
a home.   Dr. David J. Burrell has well said of
home that it is neither a prison nor a treadmill,
that it is not a place for mere disciplinary proc-
esses, that it is to be, as nearly as possibly, a
little heaven on earth—with the spirit of heaven
reigning in it.

One of the happiest conditions of childhood
exists in families where much gracious hospi-
tality is part of the household routine.   Ian
Maclaren says, "The coming of guests revives
and enriches the common life, for each has his
own tale to tell."   The preparation of the guest
chamber, of the feast, with the dainty extra
touches in linen and silver and the setting forth
of the best china, the unstinted welcome, the
kindly farewell, are elements of value in the
children's upbringing.   In some houses company is regarded as an intrusion, and dreaded,
and the children never acquire the art of graceful entertaining; in others guests are greeted
with gladness, and their pleasant presence adds
new zest to the ordinary life, and here the children learn freedom and unselfishness, and taste

the pure joy of making comfortable and at home the stranger within their gates.

Christina Rossetti, that high priestess of song whose exalted verse often soars into a realm above our lower world and seems to touch the throne of God, wrote many beautiful prayers. One of these is especially suitable for parents and children:

"Give, I pray thee, to all children grace reverently to love their parents and lovingly to obey them. Teach us all that filial duty never ends or lessens; and bless all parents in their children and children in their parents. O thou in whom the fatherless find mercy, make all orphans, I beseech thee, loving and dutiful unto thee, their true Father. Be thy will their law, thy house their home, thy love their inheritance. And, I earnestly pray thee, comfort those who have lost their children, giving mothers grace to be comforted though they are not; and grant us all faith to yield our dearest treasures unto thee with joy and thanksgiving, that where, with thee, our treasure is there our hearts may be also. Thus may we look for and hasten unto the day of union with thee, and of reunion. Amen."

CHAPTER IV

When the Young People Grow Up

When the young people, emerging from the chrysalis of childhood, put on the beautiful garments of early maturity the house is full of gay life and pleasure. There is nothing else quite like it. The coming and going of the young men who are at college or in business, and who are eager and ardent, enjoying, aspiring, building for the future, looking out from their plane of strength to the onward march of the days with never a fear nor a doubt, and the girls, so blooming, so sweet, so independent; not the fragile timid creatures who were once the poet's and the romancer's ideal of girlhood, but at once refined and vigorous, trained mentally and physically, educated along lines parallel with their brothers and fitted to be good comrades for good men on the road of life. Who can see them without enthusiasm and thankfulness?

To the parents, not yet old, who gather about

them a home bright with the charm of well-bred and affectionate young folk this period of their career is marked with a red letter. Everything revolves around these grown children. One must be allowed to go abroad to pursue a longer course of study—in Berlin, or Heidelberg, or Paris—and, though the strain has already been great, somehow father and mother find a way to help their lad that he may have the post-graduate advantages on which his soul is set. Another has resolved to study art, or to be a trained nurse, and, though the mother has been fondly anticipating the time when her daughter shall again be her daily companion, she interposes no obstacle. Edith's path is smoothed for her, and she goes bravely out upon it, followed by her mother's prayers and loving thoughts. Whatever the young people wish for, in the usual order of things, the parents endeavor to give them, and the only peril is that the average American parent shall become too self-denying and forget to consider what is due to himself.

In the household which, exceptionally favored, keeps its circle for some years unbroken the young people largely control the social life. "We do not invite our own friends any more," said a mother; "all summer in the country and all winter in town we are filling the house with their schoolmates and college mates." When school and college are over, still the young are in the ascendant, and too often the mother is gradually crowded out of her own proper place —finding herself more and more an unimportant figure, secluded in her room or seated in her rocking-chair in the back parlor.

Of course, when this happens, the mother has herself to blame. She should not consent to effacement, nor in her admiration for the sons and daughters around her lose sight of the fact that she still has rights and should be honored and considered in the household. Once in a while the young people should be left to take the helm, and the mother, fitted out with the dainty wardrobe and the new shoes and gloves which she sometimes foregoes in favor of her girls, should be sent away for an outing—a journey with her husband or a visit to her own girlhood's home. From such an experience she will return to take up the daily duties with new zest and something of the lost delight of youth.

Perhaps the most important feature in home economy, when young people are on the threshold of life, is the deciding on what they are to be in the busy activities of the world. Formerly Christian parents were prone, as they are not always now, to dedicate a son to the ministry, or a daughter to the mission field. Though, if too arbitrarily insisted upon, such pre-arrangement of a child's life might prove a great error in judgment, yet when gifts and graces accompany the development of the consecrated one it is quite possible that the path will be smoothed and the work attract the worker. But too much earthly ambition has occasionally entered into even so sacred a covenant, and the resultant disappointment might have been expected.

A father may naturally desire to have his son take up his own business or profession, and it may be a sore trial to him to discover that the boy's bent is in another direction and that he cannot fit himself into the waiting niche. When the day arrives in which serious work must be undertaken, and the youth must put his own hand to the plough, parents may give judicious and loving counsel, but their wiser part, having done this, is to stand aside and allow freedom of choice to the new comer on the stage. An artist cannot make a successful merchant, a merchant may not be a writer of books. The thing to comprehend is that all true work, undertaken in the right spirit, is honorable if done heartily, as unto the Lord.

Inevitable changes are foreshadowed in the happy days when the young people grow up. Lovers cross the old home threshold, and, while still the boys and girls seem to the parents but children, lo! they are finding their mates and beginning a new life of their own. The longer period of school and college work pushes marriage a little further on than was common in a not remote past, but so long as youth and health and goodness remain in the world love will rule it; and it is a beautiful and appropriate conclusion to the preparatory phases of the individual when he becomes the wooer, or she the wooed.

Part of a mother's obligation should be to make ready her girls and boys for the home keeping of days to come. When we indulge our young people in selfishness, through our own over fondness or over tendency to self-abnegation, we are rendering them distinctly unfit to be the custodians of others' happiness when they are beyond our hand. I do not think that a boy is less manly for knowing how to help his mother with her peculiarly feminine tasks. Why should not a boy be allowed to aid in washing dishes, in ironing, in cooking, and in sweeping, even in mending, and in stitching on the machine? Acquaintance with these homely accomplishments is highly valued in, for instance, the life of a camp, and the man who is deft and skilled in these arts, which make daily living comfortable, is popular beyond his fellows. A husband with some practical knowledge of housewifery will understand how much is demanded of his wife, and will be able to sympathize with her in the pressure of her common routine. A boy accustomed to assist his mother and the girls will not hesitate to put his shoulder to the wheel when it is his wife who requires his timely aid.

Equally, a girl should become familiar with the uses of tools, know how to drive a nail, and to turn a screw; if she live in the country, be quite independent of help as to harnessing her horse, or saddling her pony, and in every respect should be placed on a plane where she may be a comrade and friend to her brothers, and, by and by, everything his heart can wish to him whom she chooses out of the whole world to be her own.

When the hour of choosing is reached the mother and father are very deeply concerned, and it is not strange that they look with yearning and anxious eyes on those whom their children are henceforth to hold in the closest and most indissoluble relationship. Marriage is too solemn, too holy a thing, to be entered upon without a comprehension of all it involves, and to young people, determined upon the going out from the old life and into the new, it should be sacramental in character. Of course, parents may be prejudiced, and very happy unions have existed which were made in opposition to parental counsel; yet when there is opposition or hostility is it not best for the young people to wait a little time before they take the irrevocable step? Also, should they not remind themselves that, in marriage, happiness is not the only goal to be sought? People marry that they may help one another, that they may complement one another's deficiencies, that they may take part in God's work in his world. What shall be the style of Christian living in the next thirty or forty years? Only our young people can decide and answer this question.

CHAPTER V

Home Reading

"The pleasantest memory of my childhood," said a clever and brilliant man, "is the picture which I can still see, when I close my eyes, of the family group on the long winter evenings. We lived in New Hampshire, where the cold begins early and lingers late, and we were sometimes snow-bound for months, or nearly so, when the great drifts hemmed the homestead in, and we were dependent on ourselves for society with little help from neighbors—who, two or three miles away, were also in a state of siege. While frugality was studied, and our parents made the most of every dollar, there was a liberal expenditure for mental culture, and we had a goodly number of books on our shelves and several periodicals which brought to us the news of the great world and kept us in touch with all that went on beyond our mountain-circled borders.

"At evening, when the day's work was done, we gathered around the lamp, and father or

Jennie, my eldest sister, read aloud while our mother made progress with her weekly mending and the rest of us listened with eager interest. In a single winter we would read thus several volumes of history and fiction, biography or poetry, and the great names of literature were familiar on our lips."

For home reading, as considered distinctly from individual reading, a book should be one of continuous sequence, its subject sufficiently large to occupy successive days and weeks, or else it should consist of short essays, or stories, complete in themselves and easily finished at a sitting. Where people are of different ages and at different stages of advancement all cannot equally be absorbed in a volume requiring thoughtful attention, and to be grasped only by those whose previous studies have prepared them to handle it. For this reason, if a history is selected for reading aloud it should be narrative and descriptive, and popular in style rather than philosophical. A good plan is to keep for reference in a convenient place some school text-book to which one may turn for dates and names and the refreshment of recollection about battles and other pivotal events. If poetry is read,

let it be of the ballad or lyric order; few young
people would be able to listen night after night,
even if the selection were otherwise a judicious
one, to Browning's massive and magnificent
poem, "The Ring and the Book." But "Mar-
mion," or "The Lady of the Lake," or "Lord of
the Isles," could be read in a single evening, as
could Kipling's "Recessional," and a choice list
of other fine lyrics from this wonderfully vital
author of to-day. "Hervé Riel," "The Ride
from Ghent to Aix," Robert Buchanan's "Ballad
of Judas Iscariot," some ringing verse of
Whittier's or linked sweetness of Longfellow's
would profitably fill charmed evenings beside
the glowing hearth.

Discussion of what is read should be encouraged, and where a family undertakes one of the
excellent prescribed courses which are to be
found, embodying the results of scholarship and
investigation, by all means let the listeners talk
freely, and ask questions concerning what they
do not fully comprehend. Even the younger
ones by degrees find their vocabulary enlarged,
and grow familiar with rich phrases and ornate
words as they sit with their elders and partake
of a feast spread for all.

" Beside the Glowing Hearth."

In the home library there should be as of course a dictionary, and to this everyone should turn when there is uncertainty either as to the precise meaning of a word, its derivation, or its pronunciation. The best lexicons give many examples of the uses of words, culled from standard literature, and one might almost become learned who should carefully and conscientiously study a dictionary. An encyclopedia is another admirable addition to home wealth, and it were worth while to practice a thousand small economies that a stately row of such useful volumes might be always close at hand.

In the larger towns and cities, where access to a public library is not difficult, the family needs to spend less in the line of books of reference, but if the home be in the country they are indispensable. And one enjoys seeing these friendly companions and guides in the household room, where they may be sought without ceremony, and where they may act as umpires in settling any mooted point which may arise.

An atlas should be in the possession of the family, and the habit of consulting it should be encouraged. Our ideas of geography grow hazy and vague if we do not habitually have recourse to the map, and though we may stay at home, and seldom visit places distant from our own abodes, it is as well that we should know routes of travel, waterways of ocean and river, and steam communications by land, that when our foreign missionaries and our home missionaries go to their points of labor we shall be able to follow and to think of them with the definiteness which comes of assured knowledge. One cannot read the daily or weekly newspaper to-day without a frequent necessity of referring to the map, for history is making constantly, great problems are confronting the nation, maps are changing with altered political relations, and every indication points to the speedy coming in of the Kingdom of God.

I met a woman one autumn day in an isolated farmhouse six miles from the great centers of commerce. In her whole life of nearly sixty years she had not been two hundred miles from home, and of fashion and its follies, worldly splendor and its luxuries, she was entirely ignorant. But on her sitting room table were several missionary magazines, and beside them just what I am now recommending, an admirable atlas, revised and brought up to date, and I was not surprised to discover, in this gentle and home-keeping matron, one who had kept pace with the world in its progress, who was bright, animated, and keen of wit and speech, and who both prayed for Christ's cause and gave to it generously from her store.

In the purchase of books for a home library care should be exercised as to selecting the permanently valuable rather than the merely ephemeral and transient. Among those volumes which should have a place in the former classification are a Life of Christ, and when one is in doubt to whom to apply for counsel, as to which of the many in the market is the best, the natural and sensible course is to ask the pastor of your church or the teacher of your Bible class. Our Lord's life is given in all fullness in the Scriptures; its first premonitions and foreshadowings are in the Old Testament, and the four gospels are four pictures of its beautiful and matchless progress from Bethlehem to Calvary. Beyond the gospels no one is actually obliged to go for the story of the Master, but modern research and devout scholarship have thrown a clear illumination on the times

of our Lord, and on the history of nations exist-
ing and ruling when the Divine Man walked up
and down the hills and dales of Palestine. The
Christian should seek to be informed of all
which reveals the circumstances of the earthly
life of Him whose name he bears, and whose
will is his law as he goes about the business of
his own days.

Shakespeare, the Bible, the *Pilgrim's Progress,* with nothing else besides, would abundantly fill the minds and hearts of those who should
make them a daily study. The almost miracu-
lous human insight and kaleidoscopic variety
of the great dramatist are sufficient to fill many
libraries, and phrases from Shakespeare are
coin current in our common conversation. The
marvelous idyl of Bunyan is not so beloved and
studied by our young folk as it was by their pre-
decessors; but one needs only to introduce Bunyan in a home or a Sunday school to make him
immediately a chief favorite, and we should not
be at a loss when we hear reference made to
Christian, to Hopeful, and to Faithful; to
Christiana, her children, and Mercy; to Pru-
dence, Piety, and Charity; Mr. Ready-to-Halt,
Mr. Valiant-for-Truth, Mr. Standfast, and Old

Father Honest. The genius of John Bunyan is a lamp lighted for the ages, and his spell is as potent now as when first his immortal work was produced in the grim loneliness of Bedford Jail.

As for the Word of God, it is for private study not only, but always and everywhere for reading aloud in the home. I would have it read in regular order, from Genesis to Revelation, the family reading aloud, each two verses, from the father down to the wee tot whose dimpled finger traces the text while her lisping voice repeats the words after her mother. By the simple method of reading the Bible aloud at daily family prayer, we shall have a generation of church-going, God-fearing, Sabbath-observing people instead of those who are ready, in a mad pursuit of wealth or of pleasure, to forget God, and turn their backs on all which has made our country strong, prosperous, and free.

CHAPTER VI

Thrift for the Rainy Day

Thrift, a homely virtue which goes about on sturdy feet and makes no particular stir, is an eminently respectable figure though not a specially picturesque one. Thrift implies foresight, makes provision for the future, and is not resolved on the indulgence of the present at the expense of suffering to come. Far removed from the miserly quality which hoards simply for the sake of accumulation, thrift walks hand in hand with contentment, with ease of mind, and with dignified self-respect.

Pay day, however postponed, arrives as certainly as the rising of to-morrow's sun; and the thoughtlessly improvident person, who not only spends as he goes but spends more than he earns, has pay day to reckon with, and too often meets it unprepared. Then, around one's neck, weighing one to the earth, debt hangs like a millstone, and health, strength, enthusiasm, gayety, and joy in life vanish under its relentless pressure. As well may one drag a ball and chain around one's feet as walk through life fettered by the clog of debt, which seems ever larger and less manageable the longer it is carried.

Cheerful days are not compatible with obligations greater than one's financial ability to bear, and as for sleep, that vanishes from the pillow of the reckless spendthrift whose chronic condition is that of the debtor. There may be an abyss of degradation in which one is careless of debt and dishonor alike, but of this I am not speaking; for there is little difference between a debtor who ignores his debts and a thief who deliberately steals his neighbor's goods. The one is as really culpable as the other. The honest man or woman faced by debts which cannot be settled, however the situation has been brought into existence, must expect nights of misery and torture; for at midnight and at two o'clock in the morning specters of fear and anxiety haunt the spirit and rear ghostly forms in the pathway of the oncoming years.

Among the numerous causes which assist in bringing the wretchedness of poverty on the head of the bad manager the most ordinary and inevitable is a habit of living beyond one's income. Sometimes the scale of expenditure is too liberal, and the whole routine of life, so to speak, its running schedule, needs immediate alteration and rearrangement. The family live in too large a house or in too costly a neighborhood, or are too far remote from the scene of their daily labors. Perhaps the father is of a sanguine temperament and in his happy optimism is buoyant and heedless, allowing his wife and children every pleasure of the moment and living up to the full extent of his income, with no margin for extra expenses, so that when these come he is swamped, and plunged into difficulties from which he cannot easily extricate himself. In family life there are years of extraordinary costliness—as when several young people are growing up together and their education must be met, or when a prolonged season of illness or an accident and consequent surgical treatment in hospital taxes the family purse, or when for some good reason a long and expensive journey must be taken. The thrifty person keeps contingencies in view and has a margin on which to draw—a sum in bank, or other resource which is available—while his opposite, having lived too generously, is forced to over-work or to anticipate future earnings. Both of these courses are unfortunate and apt to be disastrous.

Excessive devotion to dress is a temptation to some temperaments, and, if yielded to, leads to an aftermath of mortification. Furs, silks, velvets, laces and jewels, the accompaniments of wealth, should be very moderately used by those whose income is limited. A young woman, for example, earning her own livelihood as a stenographer at fifteen dollars a week, should not wear a jacket of sealskin nor buy gems of price. Not only are these articles of elegance and beauty beyond the limitations of her pocket-book but they are in the worst possible taste and expose her to unkind criticism. Costly dress is not needful for the ordinary workingman or woman, who may be neat and well clad without extravagance, if willing to study the science of economical administration of money.

Whatever the reason of financial trouble may be one duty is self-evident, and this is to stop the leak. Ascertain where it is and at once retrieve the position by retrenchment. Practice the fine art of doing without; learn to say No to the impulse which urges you to buy what you cannot afford, or which inclines you to the recklessness of buying on credit. No one should ever have a monthly account at a store, unless he has a large and steady income, for there is nothing more deceptive than the persuasion that thirty or sixty days hence one can pay with ease the reckoning which it is impracticable to settle to-day. The habit of buying for cash only is a check upon extravagance which acts as a useful brake with most people.

A great deal of money is wasted by those who despise very small savings. In town, for instance, persons who could walk on their various errands, and to whom walking would probably be a benefit, take the trolley or the horse-car, pay five cents for a short ride, and at the day's end, or the week's end, have spent dollars in this way—dollars which could have been put to a much better use. Young girls spend more money than they like to think of in candy and in little accessories of dress which might be dispensed with. A penny saved is a penny earned, and they who look well to tiny savings will have large amounts to their credit in the long run.

Thrift for the rainy day means looking out

for old age. Nothing is sadder than the spectacle of one who has passed the halcyon time of youth and the bounds of middle age, whose working time is over and whose fund of vigor is exhausted, and to whom there has come a lonely period when kindred and friends are few. To be old and dependent on charity, or old and grudgingly sheltered and cared for by those whose conduct shows that one is in the way, is a very sorrowful lot. To lay up for the time of fragile health and of waning powers is a duty one should recognize before strength and courage and opportunity are gone.

Undoubtedly it requires an effort, and bravery almost heroic, to retrieve one's errors, to leave the large and stately mansion and live in the cottage or to change the single dwelling for the narrow flat; but of one thing most of us may be assured: the public is entirely without concern about the economies of private individuals and families, and one's own friends will care for one as truly when the manner of living is plain as when it is showy. Ostentation may invite censure, but unobtrusive simplicity wins the suffrages of all wise judges. No friends are ever lost through the accidents of wealth or the reverse, and our neighbors and acquaintances are seldom very much occupied about the externals of our lives—the way we dress, the houses we reside in, and whether we travel in the drawing-room car or modestly take our seats in the day coach.

But "men will praise thee when thou doest well for thyself" was said by one of old, and is still true in these modern days and in the end of the nineteenth century. The thrifty worker may in time become the genial person of leisure; the idler knowing nothing of prevision may never have the wherewithal for leisurely enjoyment.

Having said this, I must add that the truest thrift, to put it on the very lowest plane, accords to the Lord his share in the profits of our trade, or profession, or business. Whether or not we adhere to the old Hebrew rule and devote the tenth part of our income to the Lord, we should systematically and gratefully appropriate some part, going over our assets and receipts, and intelligently assigning to the uses of charity and religion our offering In His Name. Whosoever does this, praying for a blessing on the willing sacrifice, will never miss the satisfaction of reward given back in rich measure; pressed down and running over.

"There was one year," said a friend, "when John and I decided that we were too poor to give the Lord his tenth. Everything we touched that year failed, and discouragement met us at every turn. We have never dared since, remembering that experience and its bitterness, to defraud the Lord of his share in our substance."

Over the door of one of our world-famous philanthropists is engraved this legend: "To-day is my ain." For the rainy day not yet dawning in the gray east, for the year of the laggard step and the aching head, for the uncertainties of all the to-morrows, it is ours to provide by conscientious and diligent thrift to-day; for to-day is "oor ain," and God's.

> It isn't worth while to fret, dear,
>   To walk as behind a hearse;
> No matter how vexing things may be
>   They easily might be worse;
> And the time you spend complaining,
>   And groaning about the load,
> Would better be given to going on
>   And pressing along the road.
>
> I've trodden the hill myself, dear—
>   'Tis the tripping tongue can preach,
> But though silence is sometimes golden, child,
>   As oft there is grace in speech—

And I see, from my higher level,
  'Tis less the path than the pace
That wearies the back, and dims the eye,
  And writes the lines on the face.

There are vexing cares enough, dear,
  And to spare, when all is told;
And love must mourn its losses,
  And the cheek's soft bloom grow old;
But the spell of the craven spirit
  Turns blessing into curse,
While the bold heart meets the trouble
  That easily might be worse.

So smile at each disaster
  That will presently pass away,
And believe a bright to-morrow
  Will follow the dark to-day.
There's nothing gained by fretting;
  Gather your strength anew,
And step by step go onward, dear,
  Let the skies be gray or blue.

50

CHAPTER VII

Days of Illness

Can days of pain and weariness, of tossing to and fro in fever and sinking into depths of weakness, be accounted days of cheer?   May we preserve not merely calmness, but the sweetness of hope and the possibility of joy, in circumstances alien to everything except depression? When the body is on the rack may the soul triumph, maintaining itself in strength and heroism?

Yes, the old word of promise still abides: "Thou wilt keep him in perfect peace, whose mind is stayed on thee: because he trusteth in thee." The soul does not maintain itself but God sustains it, and the keeping is as that of the armed sentinel who paces to and fro before the gate and warns off any stealthy invader. In times of special need our Lord is specially near to his people, and so it comes to pass that many a sick chamber is as the house of Obed-edom in which the ark abode.

Said one who had known keen suffering, "The sickness of the last week was fine medicine; pain disintegrated the spirit or became spiritual. I rose. I felt that I had given to God more perhaps than an angel could—had promised him in youth that to be a blot on this world, at his command, would be acceptable. Constantly offer myself to continue the obscurest and loneliest thing ever heard of—with one proviso: his agency. Yes, love thee and all thou dost, while thou sheddest frost and darkness on every path of mine."

Once the lesson has been learned of complete submission to the Divine will that will becomes a pillow for the head and a comfort for the heart. There is no fretfulness, no resistance; only serene acquiescence, and then "He giveth songs in the night."

> "I praise thee while my days go on,
> I love thee while my days go on;
>   Through dark and dearth, through fire and frost,
>   With emptied arms and treasure lost,
> I thank thee while my days go on."

I shall never forget the look of ecstasy on the worn, sweet, illumined countenance of a beloved one who was passing through deep waters, whose fragile form was rent with anguish, and who knew, morning by morning, that relentlessly and inevitably death was encroaching upon life. I entered her chamber in the early dawn; she greeted me with her rare and beautiful smile. "Ah!" she said, "my Lord has so revealed himself to me that I have no fear, no solicitude, nothing but gladness in waiting for him. I can trust him for everything, even for the little children I am leaving to be fatherless and motherless in the world." Days and weeks wore slowly on before the silver cord was loosed, but the rapture only deepened as the earthly faded and the heavenly drew near. To all who came within her sphere that room of mortal agony was bright with a light which fell from the jasper walls.

It is not alone when death is imminent that the dear Lord can give us supremacy over pain. To one of his children it has been appointed to dwell for many years under the shadow of a malady which binds her to her couch, hand and foot. She lies there helpless as a log, lifted, turned, carried sometimes to another room, never able to perform one bodily office for husband or child; always being more or less under the bondage of a grinding poignant pain. There are hard days, and, mercifully, there are easy days, but through them all the invalid's courage and cheer is the radiant fact which keeps the home a cheerful habitation and not a gloomy cell. A friend coming in is welcomed with blithe word and happy look; the husband hears never a murmur; the son, through childhood, youth, and in early manhood, has had his mother for confidante and counselor, his education, his profession, his plans all part of her thought and part of her work, intelligently shared as to all that has concerned his development. The house, smoothly carried on in its domestic routine, has known her guiding brain if not her guiding hand, and her years of illness have been truly years of glory and victory.

Such an experience would be impossible without Christian faith, for it is forever true that

> "The healing of the seamless dress
>   Is by our beds of pain;
> We touch Him in life's throng and press,
>   And we are whole again."

William Law, whose insight was so remarkable, writing in the last century said, pithily: "If a man do not believe that all the world is as

God's family, where nothing happens by chance but all is guided and directed by the care and providence of a Being that is all love and goodness to his creatures, if a man do not believe this from his heart, he cannot be said truly to believe in God. And yet he that has this faith has faith enough to overcome the world and always be thankful to God. For he that believes that everything happens to him for the best cannot possibly complain for the want of something that is better. If therefore you live in murmurings and complaints, accusing all the accidents of life, it is not because you are a weak, infirm creature, but it is because you want the first principle of religion, a right belief in God. It is certain that, whatever seeming calamity happens to you, if you thank and praise God for it you turn it into a blessing. Could you, therefore, work miracles you could not do more for yourself than by this thankful spirit, for it heals with a word speaking, and turns all that it touches into happiness."

We should not overlook the great goodness of God which ordains that, for most of us, days of illness are episodes in the midst of days of health and activity. They interrupt us in our career, and for awhile we are laid aside, but they pass, and the tide which ebbed flows in again and we are once more able to go to the office or the shop, to sit at the head of the table, to engage in the multitudinous affairs of our lives. During the period of inaction it is well for us if we have been able to lay everything in the kind hands of God, to trust everything to him, sure that he will not appoint us one bitter drop too much.

The real test comes to us when not only is our illness the occasion of pain to us personally, but when, if prolonged, it brings great weariness to our caretakers and perhaps entails privation upon them, in the loss of means which the bread-winner earns when in health. To feel that there is no time to be ill is to know a very keen, knife-like thrust of anguish. Yet here too the childlike heart will breathe "Thy will be done," and will repose in confidence on the pledge that "all things work together for good to those who love God."

We must sometimes be ready to cry,

> "But if this weariness hath come
> A present from on high,
> Teach me to find the hidden wealth
> That in its depths may lie."

One of the most difficult tasks and heaviest burdens ever laid upon a believing soul is to see the suffering of little children. When pain comes to an infant too young to tell what hurts and where the hurt is, when its arresting presence stops the mirth of the growing boy and shuts down like a heavy curtain on the brightness of the young girl, we, who can only minister, who cannot avert the ill, nor take it away and bear it ourselves, find it terribly hard to be cheerful and composed. Childhood ought to be so free from sickness, so full of elasticity and delight, that suffering laid upon its shoulders appears to us as an anachronism. Happily, children accept without murmuring whatever the day brings them, and for that very reason they recover more rapidly from any transient malady than their elders do. And for our children as for ourselves, in our days of the darkness and of the light, we must ask grace for the day and believe and hope and wait, sure that in the hottest furnace there will walk with us One like unto the Son of God.

> "The folded hands seem idle.
> If folded at His word
> 'Tis a holy service, trust me,
> In obedience to the Lord."

"Among so many can he care?
Can special love be everywhere?
A myriad homes, a myriad ways,
And God's eye over every place?
I asked. My soul bethought of this:
In that same very place of his
Where he hath put and keepeth you
God hath no other thing to do."

Invalids frequently look back to convalescence as a time of peculiar blessedness. The difference between convalescence and extreme illness in the initiative is often so very slight that a physician or a nurse only can state, with anything like assurance, whether the tide has really turned or whether it is still ebbing out toward eternity. If it has turned, and, ever so slowly, life is flowing back, then there may be for a while no improvement sufficiently marked to be admitted as such by the unprofessional eye. In convalescence one sometimes measures progress by weeks, when by days there is apparently none to mark. Scanning the past seven days or fourteen days there is noted an increase of strength, ability to take more nourishment, less irritation of nerves, less sensitive quivering at a slight noise, presently a little more desire to know what is going on, and soon a wish to see inquiring friends. This last step must be taken with

great caution, and visitors from the world outside accepted with wise discrimination, while in
the hand to hand conflict between vitality and
morbid tendency the forces of the former are
gaining the ascendant.

In the early stages of convalescence a patient
requires very tender and judicious care. There
must be no relaxation of vigilance, no intermis-
sion of the sentries on guard, for a small indis-
cretion, an unmeant blunder, may occasion that
dreaded condition of affairs, a relapse; a thing
to be scrupulously avoided, since the victim has
not now the reserves on which to draw, as he had
when originally taken ill. In convalescence one
must make haste slowly. Tide over by every
possible means that phase of returning health
when even a statesman, in his invalid weakness,
may behave like a spoiled baby. Is it never
coming back, the old independence of action,
the old swiftness of thought, the old exhilara-
tion in work, and rapture in being alive? Perhaps the despair and depression express themselves in a curtness or brusqueness alien to the
manner of the person in health, but pardoned by
attendants and friends who know that it is
merely incidental to weakness, and that it will

be transient. Now, when the room is flooded with sunshine and radiant with flowers, when a child's foot is allowed to cross the threshold, and a child's sweet voice is heard beside the bed, the crossness, for it is just that, passes away, and the invalid begins to enjoy the returning days, each laden for him or her with new gifts and graces.

What gratitude we owe to that minister of love the trained nurse, a product of nineteenth century wisdom. There have always been women described as born nurses; women with cool hands, deft and skillful, and with that faculty for care-taking which is brought to its highest water-mark under the discipline of a nurses' school. But our modern nurse is fortunate in being able to economize her own strength; she is not disturbed by the emotional strain which wears on wife and mother; she is the doctor's obedient instrument, and in her best estate becomes the prized and honored friend of the family.

In the old days God sent his angels oft
  To men in threshing-floors, to women pressed
With daily tasks ; they came to tent and croft,
  And whispered words of blessing and of rest.

Trustful To-morrows

Not mine to guess what shape those angels wore,
    Nor in what voice they spoke, nor with what grace
They brought the dear love down that evermore
    Makes lowliest souls its best abiding-place.

But in these days I know my angels well;
    They brush my garments on the common way,
They take my hand, and very softly tell
    Some bit of comfort in the waning day.
And though their angel names I do not ken,
    Though in their faces human love I read,
They are God-given to this world of men,
    God-sent to bless it in its hours of need.

Child, mother, dearest wife, brave hearts that take
    The rough and bitter cross, and help me bear
Its heavy weight when strength is like to break,
    God bless you all, our angels unaware!

CHAPTER VIII

Comfort in Sorrow

"Into each life some rain must fall."

Sorrow sooner or later visits every one. It may be of one or another variety; it may be grief over the dead or distress over the living. A child gone astray is a far greater source of sorrow than a child asleep in the cemetery. The trouble which one has over the living is never finished; it rises up with one at morning, accompanies him all day, and lies down with him at night. What form it shall next take depends on so many possible combinations of temptation or opportunity that they who endure this special form of trial seldom feel secure; they are in dread of some new feature, some dénouement worse than the last.

"When my darling boy died after a few hours of frightful illness I was prostrated in the very dust," said a mother. "My whole world lay about me in ruins. The narrow grave in which we laid him blotted the sunshine from our sky, and I remember three lines of poetry which I

read that mournful summer, and which kept
recurring to me,

> 'His part in all the pomp that fills
> The circuit of the summer hills
> Is that his grave is green.'

For years I rejected consolation, and turned my
back on every solace; I was angry with God,
who had dared to snatch away my son. That
was the worst part of it—the hard, cold, bitter
spot in my heart, and the sense of absence from
my Heavenly Father. I have learned now that
there are griefs to which mine was nothing.

"My friend, whose son and mine were schoolmates, has spent months in trying to free him
from a vile accusation. She believes him to be
innocent, as I do, but around his feet a network
of incriminating circumstantial evidence has
been woven, and he is in prison, his name de-
famed, his home broken up, his career ruined,
and apparently there is no way out of the difficulty. The only thing which buoys that mother
up is her firm belief that her boy is innocent;
there are mothers who have no reason for such
a trust when their sons are accused. I have
reached a place where I can say 'Thank God for
my darling in heaven!'"

Of whatever nature our particular grief may be there is balm for it in the Gilead of God's great dispensary. The sad-faced woman whom I met carrying roses to lay on a mound in that beautiful God's acre at Savannah, where the weird gray moss hangs from the trees and the jasmine lights its golden star above the silent sleepers, smiled in my face as she said, "Robbie never had a moment to rest before. He can rest now." Mrs. Browning was in the right when she interpreted the feeling of thousands who are bereaved,

> "Well done of God to halve the lot,
>   And give her all the sweetness ;
> To us, the empty room and cot ;
>   To her, the heaven's completeness."

If we can but be unselfish our grief for the dead is cheated of its sting ; and in our grief for the living there is usually at least one mitigation, that of hope for a brighter day. "It is better farther on," we sing, and take courage.

A man honored and beloved by all his friends died suddenly some years ago in a New York hospital. He had been in receipt of an ample salary and had few personal extravagances. There seemed no reason why he should die in

debt, yet, when he was gone, it was discovered
that to the charity of friends and acquaintances
he must owe the six feet of earth in which he
was to lie. No one could understand the situation or explain it, but after a while the fact
transpired that for years he had been supporting a relative, a man of education and native
refinement who had taken to drink, who had
fallen lower and lower until all kinsmen but this
one had abandoned him, who had finally degen-
erated into a social outcast and a tramp. The
drain on the man's resources had been constant, and he had deprived himself of almost
everything that he might assist his weaker
brother, and finally he had dropped down beneath a load too heavy for him to bear. This
was a day by day torture, so cheerfully endured
that its very existence had not been suspected.

In sorrow, whatever it be, the natural temper of the mind must be considered; its power
of reaction from the first despair, and its elasticity or its sluggishness. A mercurial person
resists melancholy, and fights against it. A perfectly well and vigorous person has in physical
strength an armor against morbid grief. Comfort comes to some of us in every pulsation of

the heart, in every waft of the breeze, in every sunset cloud and blooming flower. Others are obstinately sorrowful, and, against their own will, find their hearts as heavy as lead—receiving comfort only from time, which blunts the edge of the sharpest wounds.

Duty, however, points to unselfishness in sorrow. No matter how desperate the situation, how forlorn the day, we have no right to include in our own misery those we meet, strangers, or visitors, or children. For the sake of others we must arise and eat bread, and go about our daily work and make the most of what still remains. To gather up the fragments that nothing may be lost is still the divine injunction, and it is incumbent on us all.

The effort to look and speak cheerfully, and the endeavor to make others happy, will usually be successful in bringing relief to our own bosoms. The getting out of self is absolutely essential. I shall always remember a Christian gentlewoman who came on the appointed day of its meeting to a board in which she held an important office. Only three days had elapsed since there had been a funeral at her home, and we had followed to Greenwood the form of her son, laid low in his early maturity. "The Lord's work must be done," she said, and calmly, without wavering and without delay, took up what he had appointed her.

"Blessed are they that mourn: for they shall be comforted," said the Master, and somehow, at the core of the deepest desolation, there is a honey of sweetness in the thought of that pledge of blessing. For by whom are we to be comforted? By no human agency alone; if by human means, they are but channels through which our God will move. In our extremity the compassionate Jesus will himself loose our bonds and give us freedom and support.

One of the dearest elderly women I ever knew after the decease of an idolized daughter found alleviation of her loneliness in taking up the daughter's work. The young lady had been untiring in her devotion to an orphanage—visiting it frequently, teaching classes of the little ones, raising money for its endowment, and personally placing the children in homes when they were ready to leave the fostering care of the institution. Everything the daughter had done, in her plenitude of youth and fullness of vigor, the mother did in her lessened strength and greater age, and her gentle face and slender figure in its trailing robes of black were soon familiar in haunts which they had previously not known. In her loving ministries she was abundantly blessed, and there came to her such a sense of companionship with the one who was gone as she could have found in no other way.

A certain household where sons were as olive plants around the table had one little daughter, who was so petted and prized and made much of that she was almost the corner stone of the domestic edifice. Blanche was the darling of parents and brothers, the youngest of the flock, a lovely girl whose future loomed up in unclouded splendor. She could ride, swim, drive, hold her own in any sport and in any study, and her beauty was like that of an unfolding flower. No expense was spared for Blanche, and she had not an unfulfilled wish in the world.

Suddenly as if lightning had flashed from a clear sky a fatal sickness smote her, and she was not, for God had taken her.

> "There is no flock, however watched and tended,
>   But one dead lamb is there;
> There is no household, howsoe'er defended,
>   But has one vacant chair."

"One Little Daughter."

Very blank was the empty space, very silent
the house, very sweeping the sorrow, in the home
from which Blanche had been snatched. What
did the parents do? Just this. As soon as they
could rally from the shock and gather themselves together they computed the amount they
had spent each year for Blanche, the amount
they would probably have spent in the years of
her early womanhood, and they consecrated that
sum to the education of another girl of her age,
and to the salary of a missionary woman in a
foreign station where Blanche was interested.
And so they kept her little candle burning, .
though they sat in the dark.

A sorrow for some of us is found in the opening of our eyes to our own limitations. There
was a golden day when we felt that defeat and
retreat were terms we could never understand.
Our plans were made for success. With failure
we should never have aught to do. But the
onward march has seen us lagging in the rear,
where we anticipated pushing forward in the
van. We are aware that we cannot keep the
pace that our contemporaries have taken; we
must instead walk softly, and, not able to do all
we would, we must do what we can. In this

condition let us cease to fret, for even here there is comfort in the thought that "they also serve who only stand and wait." As in the old days an equal division of spoil was the portion of those who tarried by the stuff as of those who went to the field and fought the foe, so, to-day, God's rewards are distributed impartially to all who do his will, whether in the open contest or in the quiet of the curtained room.

How rich a comfort have those derived who, being blessed by God with large means, have consecrated them to the uses of humanity, linking the college, the hospital bed, the gymnasium, the nurses' home, or the library, with the name of some one who has a new Christ-given name in the Jerusalem that is above. The broad university, forever dispensing liberal culture and scientific knowledge to eager youth, and giving them educational opportunities in their poverty which the millionaire's purse were scarcely large enough to buy, is a white stone erected for the love of a son gone home to the better land and sorely missed here. Every small crippled child treated in a certain hospital bed owes its relief and cure to the undying sorrow of a mother from whose arms one summer day two bonny little ones slipped away. Broken-hearted parents saw their splendid boy close his eyes on the lights of earth and their own way grew so black that they groped in it as if blind, till a star arose to show them the path and they heard a voice saying, "I [who have taken him] will come again, and receive you unto myself." The fruit of that hour is a superb gymnasium for the Young Men's Christian Association of which their son was a member, and so long as happy-hearted young people shall enjoy its benefits it will be a testimony of one Christ-like method of finding comfort in sorrow, the peace under the deep sea, though the billows are in agitation above.

IF CHRIST WERE HERE TO-NIGHT

If Christ were here to-night and saw me tired,
  And half afraid another step to take,
I think he'd know the thing my heart desired,
  And ease that heart of all its throbbing ache.

If Christ were here, in this dull room of mine
  That gathers up so many shadows dim,
I am quite sure its narrow space would shine,
  And kindle into glory around him.

If Christ were here I might not pray so long:
  My prayer would have such little way to go;
'T would break into a burst of happy song,
  So would my joy and gladness overflow.

If Christ were here to-night I'd touch the hem
  Of his fair, seamless robe, and stand complete
In wholeness and in whiteness; I, who stem
  Such waves of pain to kneel at his dear feet.

If Christ were here to-night I'd tell him all
  The load I carry for the ones I love—
The blinded ones, who grope and faint and fall,
  Following false guides, nor seeking Christ above.

If Christ were here! Ah, faithless soul and weak,
  Is not the Master ever close to thee?
Deaf is thine ear, that can'st not hear him speak;
  Dim is thine eye, his face that can not see.

Thy Christ is here, and never far away;
  He entered with thee when thou camest in;
His strength was thine through all the busy day:
  He knew thy need, he kept thee pure from sin.

Thy blessed Christ is in thy little room;
  Nay, more—the Christ himself is in thy heart;
Fear not; the dawn will scatter darkest gloom,
  And heaven will be of thy rich life a part.

CHAPTER IX

Looking Forward

From the hour when the pilgrimage begins
there is a continual looking forward, a reaching
out of powers and endeavors to a goal ever
beckoning the ardent soul. Indeed before the
human being takes his place in the great world
armies there is an intense and sacred expectation clinging to him, inwoven in the very fibers
of his mental and physical consciousness. In
one most important though altogether hidden
period of existence, the pre-natal, the little child
of God who is presently to put on immortality
is the object of devout and loving anticipation
in the home, and to one person, the mother, is a
wonder and a joy in the months of looking forward while the babe in her womb is in sanctuary. Never is a woman so hallowed, so lifted
above the ordinary plane, so beautiful, as when,
the glory of her coming motherhood upon her,
she holds herself away and apart from every de-
basing thought, keeps herself serene and pure,
for the sake of the child whom she feels but can-

not see. Keeps herself? Nay, rather, in these long, hushed, waiting days she is kept, trusting in God, from evil thoughts and from fear, from petty irritations and flurries of anger, while she is often rapt in meditation and is wistful that her divine Friend and Master may enter into her home and abide with her there. For in these days of looking forward the mother too is in sanctuary, sheltered by the tender watching angels, hearing symphonies of heaven, and communing much with the Most High.

Strange, when the anticipation is so sweet and the reality so blessed, that there should ever be reluctant maternity, that the days when the mother is brooding over her nursery should ever be aught but cheerful!

Mothers have the monopoly of sacred joy in the dear looking forward, wistful, wondering, waiting till the sacred hour of birth arrives, and they greet their new darling. Nothing else in the world is like this. In a recently published autobiography there is a very touching passage in which a wife, seeing her husband's life drifting out day by day and fearing he might go before he saw his unborn child, a thing which actually happened, often strayed into a little

room in the Pitti Palace in Florence where
hung a famous picture of the Visitation. Lonely, a stranger in a strange land with a great
anguish staring her in the face, Margaret Oliphant said, "It seemed to do me good to go and
look at these two women, the tender old Elizabeth, and Mary with all the awe of her coming
motherhood upon her. I had little thought of
all that was to happen to me before my child
came, but I had no woman to go to, to be comforted, except these two." This is a touching
revelation of the way art may prove God's
messenger, in a crisis, just as Nature so often
does. All the rose-strewn path of childhood is
for mothers a looking forward, from the first
toddling steps to the going to school, then onward to the choosing of a profession. The present is but the foothold by which the mother
climbs to the next level in advance.

But we look forward in many other fields.
Without this quality, which acts as a saving salt,
we might stagnate. Things would not be worth
while; for nobody lives only for food and raiment, and for the festivity of the hour alone, if
he or she possesses the instincts which are the
birthright of an immortal being. "We eat and

drink and to-morrow we die" is the hopeless out-cry of the skeptic who, with Omar Khayyam, sees in the sky only an inverted bowl under which the generations creep and crawl to noth-ingness. Not so with those who feel the power of the world to come pressing them round in this time of preparation. For them the looking for-ward always crosses the river and mounts the heights on the other side.

Is there anything in literature more winsome and charming than the looking forward of Mar-garet Ogilvy and her son, told in the inimitable manner of one of our greatest men of genius:

"Mother, the little girl in my story wears a magenta frock and a white pinafore."

"You minded that! But I'm thinking it wasna a lassie in a pinafore you saw in the long parks of Kinnordy, it was just a gey done auld woman."

"It was a lassie in a pinafore, mother, when she was far away, but when she came near it was a gey done auld woman."

"And a fell ugly one!"

"The most beautiful one I shall ever see!"

"I wonder to hear you say it. Look at my wrinkled auld face."

"It is the sweetest face in all the world."

"See how the rings drop off my poor wasted finger."

"There will always be some one nigh, mother, to put them on again."

"Ay will there! Well I know it. Do you mind how when you were but a bairn you used to say, 'Wait till I'm a man, and you'll never have a reason for greeting again'?

"You used to coming running into the house to say, 'There's a proud dame going down the Marywell brae in a cloak that is black on one side and white on the other; wait till I'm a man and you'll have one the very same.' And when I lay on gey hard beds you said, 'When I'm a man you'll lie on feathers.' You saw nothing bonny, you never heard of my setting my heart on anything, but what you flung up your head and cried, 'Wait till I'm a man.' You fair shamed me before the neighbors; and yet I was windy, too. And now it has all come true like a dream. I can call to mind not one little thing I ettled for in my lusty days that hasna been put into my hands in my auld age."

Was there not to the son of Margaret Ogilvy an unutterable gratitude of heart that his looking forward for his beloved mother's welfare had been so fulfilled, that he had been able to do for her in manhood what the leal laddie had planned in childish days?

Most husbands and wives must begin their united partnership in the day of small things. They have their fortunes to make, and so they set out, if they are sensible, in the unpretending little home with the very simple furnishing, and with no attempt at gorgeous draperies, costly rugs, or lavish display. Their careful economies, their conscientious use of every dollar, their investing for a future day, are noble and honorable, and yet more: they are satisfying and delightful. What pleasure of the millionaire in buying the picture he fancies in a gallery, drawing his check, and thinking no more about it, can for a moment compare with the sense of achievement, of victory gained, which is the crowning joy of a young couple who for a year have been saving up to secure a coveted painting for their walls? How often have they strolled past the dealer's shop and gazed into his window! How their hearts went down, down, into the depths when once that window failed to hold their picture—when another had replaced it.

Trembling and disturbed they ventured in, to ask whether it had been bought and sent away; and how hope revived when they saw it still within their grasp, if only the little sums put by would mount up faster. Their children in days to come will wonder why papa and mamma, lovers yet, so often sit hand in hand on the sofa and look at the old picture brought home when the eldest born was a baby. Ah! they cannot fathom what love and faith and hope meant to their parents in the cheery days when they worked together for their home building and money was scarce.

Above all other serviceable gifts is a capacity for looking forward when one meets reverses. The ship is going on under full sail, and everything is favorable for a successful voyage, when, lo! a cloud appears on the horizon, a gale rises, the storm gathers and breaks. Our shores are strewn with the wreckage of vessels that were only yesterday faring on bravely toward their desired haven. In some cases the wreck is final; the sailor never tries to make another port. In others, the mariner with steady eye and splendid courage builds a boat—perhaps of driftwood, if he can do no more—runs up a rag of canvas, looks aloft for help and goes on to retrieve every disaster and come gallantly home at last. Blessed is the disposition in which there is the ability to rebound; which is not crushed by calamity, but takes its courage in both hands and goes on.

"Speak unto the children of Israel, that they go forward," came ringing from the skies, when the mountains and the desert and the sea were all presenting obstacles in the path of their progress. Since he who watcheth Israel neither slumbers nor sleeps, why should we not always listen for that command and not only look, but go, forward through all the days?

CHAPTER X

Music at Home

FORTY years ago, here in America, our
notions of music were very primitive. A piano
was considered part of the essential furnishings
of a comfortable home, and one or two of the
daughters of the household took music lessons
as a matter of course. Women whose hair is
silvered and who have put on the amplitude of
later middle life remember what a trial those
music lessons were, recall the practicing which
held them rigidly fast while their brothers were
out on the hills playing ball or skating over the
frozen lake. The half hours and the hours were
scrupulously exacted, careful aunts and mothers
watching the clock when the young girl herself
had not a conscience to be trusted, and by degrees the book of exercises was somehow finished, the earliest novitiate was passed, and the
performer took pieces—battles, marches, polkas,
and variations. Once in a while a girl with real
musical taste and decided talent persevered and
became a musician, but as a rule the hardly-won

skill was soon lost, laid aside as a useless tool, soon rusted, when marriage or maturity arrived.

One good thing resulted from the somewhat crude efforts of that bygone period, and that was a great deal of innocent sociability and gayety in home and neighborhood life. There was in every company a young woman who could play. Frequently there were several young women whose playing was agreeable, and the piano on long winter evenings was the natural rallying center of the domestic circle. Friends happened in, and there was singing. A little music enlivened the routine of work. Father enjoyed it, lying back in his easy chair with the weekly paper, forgotten, on his lap. Mother felt great pride in her daughter's accomplishment; it meant poetry and brightness and beauty to her, redeeming her years from the gradual narrowing in of their interests. If a brother was tempted away from home, lured by evil associates, apt to go astray, there was always the resource of music to keep him in safe bounds; his sister and his friends' sisters could weave around him their innocent spells and make home so attractive that the magic of vice fell away and lost its malevolent power. Passing down a village street one heard the tinkle of the "four and twenty black slaves and the four and twenty white" in every parlor, and a new song, a new arrangement of a motive, was the theme of conversation among maidens fair as they matched worsteds and silks and exchanged dress patterns.

Who fancies that lessons for a year or two are now sufficient to turn out a skilled musician? Who would be satisfied with the cursory acquaintance and slovenly technique of those curiously simple days? We are now aware that art is a jealous mistress, that he or she who would become proficient at her shrine must lead a laborious life and give her utmost devotion. To play even fairly well one must sacrifice many other advantages, and few people are contented, in our more advanced condition of scientific knowledge, in our more enlightened view point of criticism and intelligence, to play at all unless they can play well.

The result is admirable in one aspect. Many girls have time to cultivate their physical health, have opportunity for outdoor air and recreation, who once spent their morning or their afternoon hours, when freed from school, in a wrestle with scales and finger exercises. But something has gone from home, and its quiet enjoyment, which might well come back. There is a vanished joy.

May we not plead for a middle course, for the use of facility, even if it be not of the very highest, and for the return of simple music as a part of our everyday life?

Nothing is more refreshing than a half hour of song when the work of the day is over. For the family to gather at the close of the evening and sing the dear old favorites, such as "Abide with me," "Lead, kindly Light," and "Sun of my soul, thou Saviour dear," is to send all to rest with a benediction. There are popular melodies, rollicking college songs, tender old ballads, which have a melody and grace of their own, and which make a swift and tender appeal to the sentiments of faith, love, and loyalty. Our patriotic and martial strains should be sung often in every home, and school, and church. While, so far as we can, we should seek the best we should not scorn second-best in our own performances, if that is all which lies within our reach.

I would have girls learn, what is after all not so simple a thing as it sounds, the accomplishment of playing an accurate accompaniment to the songs of another. A good accompanist is a social benefactress, and on occasion she may make her skill pecuniarily profitable. Then, too, I would have all players assiduously cultivate a musical memory, so that they may be set free from the bondage of notes, and I would also like them to be swift and sure sight readers, so that at an instant's call they could play a score and relieve the embarrassment of any occasion where an expected performer had fallen out of line.

I am not speaking here of the subtle and sweet interpretations of the great masters, nor of those who have learned to play as professionals do. I am asking only that as a contribution to the gayety of life we may still have our home performers.

There is a lovely poem of Frances Ridley Havergal which illustrates what I mean:

> "Sing to the little children
>   And they will listen well,
> Sing grand and holy music,
>   For they can feel its spell.

*   *   *   *   *

"I remember, late one evening,
　How the music stopped, for, hark!
Charlie's nursery door was open,
　He was calling in the dark.
'O, no! I am not frightened,
　And I do not want a light;
But I cannot sleep for thinking
　Of the song you sang last night.
Something about a "valley"
　And "make rough places plain,"
And, "Comfort ye," so beautiful!
　O, sing it me again.'

"Sing in the deepening twilight
　When the shadow of eve is nigh,
And the purple and golden pinions
　Fold o'er the western sky.
Sing in the silver silence
　While the first moonbeams fall;
So shall your power be greater
　Over the hearts of all.
Sing till you bear them with you
　Into a holy calm,
And the sacred tones have scattered
　Manna and myrrh and balm.

"Sing that your song may gladden;
　Sing like the happy rills
Leaping in sparkling blessing,
　Fresh from the breezy hills.
Sing that your song may silence
　The folly and the jest,
And the 'idle word' be banished
　As an unwelcome guest.
Sing that your song may echo
　After the strain is past—
A link of the love-wrought cable
　That holds some vessel fast.

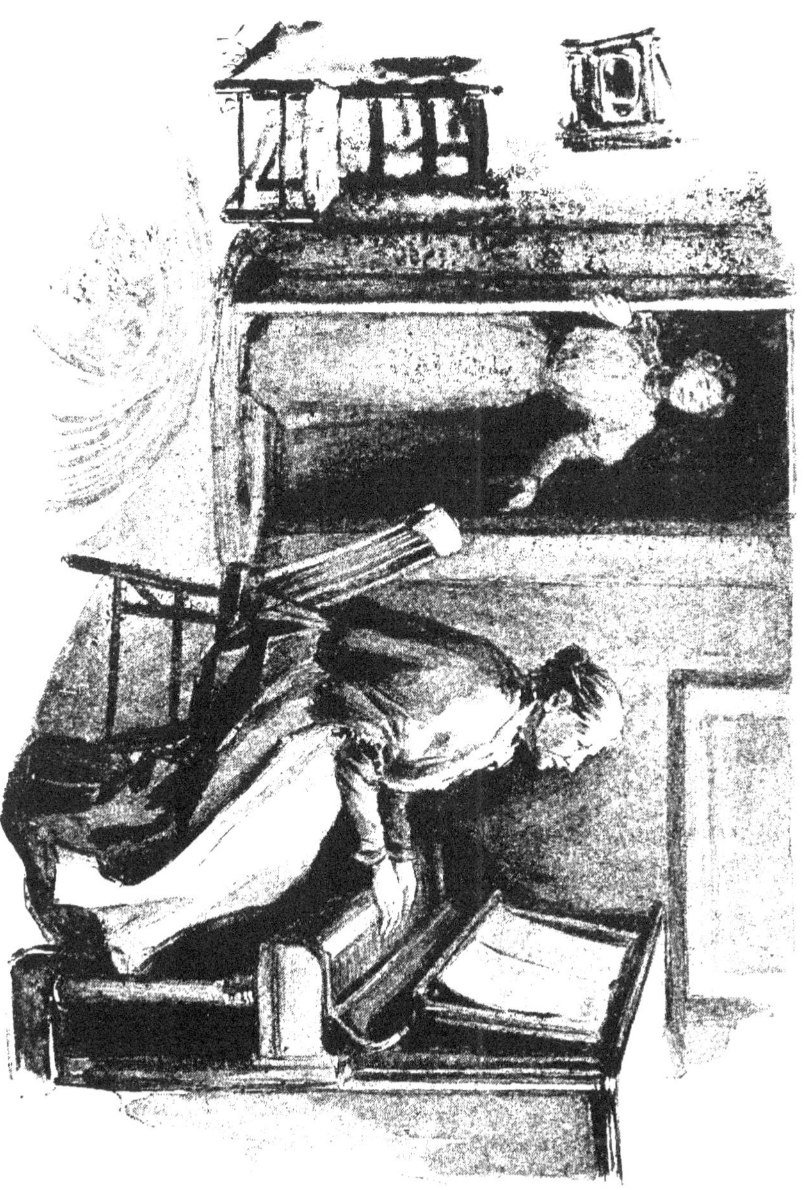

"Sing to the tired and anxious;
  It is yours to fling a ray,
Passing indeed, but cheering,
  Across the rugged way.

"When you long to bear the message
  Home to some troubled breast,
Then sing with loving fervor,
  'Come unto Me and rest!'
Or, would you whisper comfort
  When words bring no relief,
Sing how 'He was despisèd,
  Acquainted with our grief,'
And aided by His blessing
  The song may win its way
Where speech had no admittance,
  And change its night to day."

When the sweet singer who wrote these stanzas was lying in the hush of her last illness she was heard to whisper, "Splendid to be so near the gates of heaven!" "So beautiful to go!" With her failing voice, hardly more than a sigh, she breathed forth one of her best loved hymns, "Jesus, I will trust thee," to a tune of her own composing.

"Then," said her sister, "she looked up steadfastly as if she saw the Lord! and surely nothing less heavenly could have reflected such a glorious radiance upon her face. For ten minutes we watched that almost visible meeting with her King, and her countenance was so glad, as if she were already talking to him. Then she tried to sing, but after one sweet, high note, her voice failed, and as her brother commended her soul to the Redeemer's hand she passed away!"

I have purposely introduced this little account of the last scene of a beautiful earthly life, because it seems plain to me that our young people might make so much use, if they would, of a ministry of music in their daily life. I do not say in their religious life, for there can be no separation, in a truly consecrated heart, between one part of duty and another. Every bit of life is hallowed if indeed we belong to the King; and all service rendered to him, in whatsoever place, must be fit to ask his blessing upon. If Christ were sitting in our drawing-room, what sort of music should we play? What songs should we sing? That is always a true test, and whosoever is willing to bring to it any question of right or wrong will speedily find it answered and, once for all, settled.

CHAPTER XI

OF BEAUTY AND ITS CHARM

A VERY wise woman once said that "the greatest of blessings for some people would be to learn to accept themselves and their gifts. If they could stand apart from themselves awhile and see their becoming points much of their repining would be dropped." Every thing and every body is beautiful in its season. There is a wholesome plainness that accords with domestic life and natural surroundings, as the bark of trees relieves their green. The color of health and the gentleness and sweetness that come of a conquered self are elements of beauty that make any face tolerable.

How dear are the faces of those that have watched our childhood, with whom we have grown up so closely that feature and form have lost their significance and we really do not know whether they are homely or not, and see only the love that lives in them.

I often wonder why women care so much about their looks. Youth has a rare perfection belonging to itself. To be young is to be lovely, unless the young face be spoiled by ill temper or self will, or an expression of contempt or disdain. A clear pure complexion, bright eyes, smooth hair, are within the grasp of anyone who lives according to the laws of health, eats nourishing food, takes sufficient sleep, and bathes with regularity. Water, air, food, exercise, these are the requirements of health, and health is the basis of beauty.

Beyond this the mind enters in as a factor, and the mind not only governs the body but pervades it as a lamp scatters the darkness in a room. A lovely soul makes a lovely face.

I have seen a young woman reared in the close surrounding atmosphere of a tenement neighborhood, a neighborhood where eighteen hundred people were packed and crowded into one short block. That girl has known nothing of sweetness and light. Her ears have heard coarse words, her eyes have seen dirt and disorder, she has known drunkenness and brutality, meanness and sordidness, through her childhood and youth. In her countenance lived no refinement and little brightness. Even the usual prettiness of girlhood had not stamped her form and figure, bowed by much carrying about of heavy babies while she was a child and by strenuous labor in a hot factory when she first grew up.

Brought into the pleasant and serene atmosphere of a Girls' Club, taught that the world held friends, and brought to know the best Friend, I have seen the roughness and coarseness drop from such a nature, as a withered husk from a flower, and the bud open in strange purity and fragrance. Day by day there has dawned a new charm in the features, which have visibly softened; day by day a lovelier beauty has been marked, as gentleness replaced rudeness and love did its mellowing work.

No one has ever engaged in a hand to hand conflict with poverty and sin without seeing that, as Christ's dear ones were rescued from the adversary, there came to them a wonderful improvement of personality as part of their redemption.

In our cheerful outlook on life we must not forget this dominance of mind over body, nor ignore the potentiality of the spiritual over the material. And it is beneath the attention of no sensible woman—or man, for that matter—

to care enough for dress to make dress appropriate to every occasion. The fashion of the hour allows much latitude; we may be costumed in accordance with convenience and yet not outrage public opinion. Our girls go where they will in short skirts and thick boots; even our elderly women adopt a toilette for storms and rainy weather at which the conservative used to shake very doubtful heads. A little study of colors and shapes, above all an exquisite neatness and tidiness, will go far toward making women ideally charming in their homes.

We who are young are insensibly making the women we are to be by and by. The girl of twenty is the artist in whose hands lies her future self of forty; the woman of forty, and she alone, can indicate the woman of sixty. Why are women so desperately shy of lines and wrinkles? These are not necessarily defacements; they are often enhancements of charm. Nothing can possibly be more pitiful than an elderly face in which the lines are painfully smoothed out by anxious massage and the use of cosmetics. Life should write its history in every woman's face. The comeliness of youth is of another order than the attractiveness of a later period. A very plain young woman may be handsome in middle age, and a singularly beautiful girl may grow ordinary and inconspicuous when old. In the eyes of husband, father, brother and lover beauty is not a mere affair of tint and air; it is freely accorded to those who make for them the sunshine of their days.

To the Turk, a mountain of flesh with folds of fat hanging from her chin is eminently pleasing. For the Chinese, the spectacle of an enameled lady tottering on tiny deformed feet fills perfectly his strange ideal. We look for dignity, composure, and gentleness, and as their fitting accompaniment expect symmetry and grace.

Ruskin sums up the idea of the modern woman in a famous passage: "The woman's power is for rule, not for battle, and her intellect is not for invention or creation, but for sweet ordering, arrangement and decision. She sees the qualities of things, their claims and their places. Her great function is Praise; she enters into no contest, but infallibly judges the crown of contest. By her office and place she is protected from all danger and temptation. The man in his rough work in the open world must encounter all peril and trial; to him, therefore, the failure, the offense, the inevitable error; often he must be wounded or subdued, often misled, and always hardened. But he guards the woman from all this; within his house, as ruled by her, unless she herself has sought it, need enter no danger, no temptation, no cause of error or offense. This is the true nature of home; it is the place of peace; the shelter not only from all injury but from all terror, doubt and division.

"In so far as it is not this it is not home. So far as the anxieties of the outer life penetrate into it, and the inconsistently-minded, unknown, unloved, or hostile society of the outer world is allowed by either husband or wife to cross the threshold, it ceases to be home; it is then only a part of that outer world which you have roofed over and lighted fire in. But so far as it is a sacred place, a vestal temple, a temple watched over by the household gods before whose faces none may come but those whom they can receive with love, so far as it is this, and roof and fire are types only of a nobler shade and light—shade as of the rocks in the weary land, and light as of the Pharos in the stormy sea—so far it vindicates the name and fulfills the praise of home."

What has this to do with beauty? Everything. For beauty is harmony, beauty is proportion, beauty is a rhythm in which there is no discord. When one meets a thoroughly poised and balanced nature one meets beauty, and it is instantly recognized and immediately begins its work of beneficence.

One finds it difficult and elusive when one endeavors to give it definition. Witness the laborious efforts of certain novelists who have tried to depict their heroines, telling of features, skin, hair, and eyes, and leaving one as ignorant at the end as at the beginning of the real appearance of the subject. So truth-telling a medium as the camera is often misleading, for beauty resides in expression rather than in externals which grief may corrode, illness mar, and the advance of time destroy.

"I have never before met people with such light in their faces," said one who entered a company where Christ's love was the pervading note. The blessedness and the purity of their high communion so exalted them that the very lines of their countenances were ennobled.

CHAPTER XII

MOTHERS AND SONS

THE mother was tall and fair and blue-eyed, a well-balanced, strong and cheery woman. Her boys were like her; her daughter repeated the traits of her poet father, and was slight, and dark, and given to day dreams. It was a happy household, full of interest, never dull, never two days alike; it had as many changes and varying aspects as the sky. Around it, set in its beautiful garden of flowers—roses, lilies, violets, pansies, every sweet blooming and perfumed blossom you could imagine—stretched the endless Florida forests, the straight pines standing solemnly like sentries, the weird moss draping the branches, the red bird and the mocking bird flitting to and fro.

The family were always poor, and often they had no balance in any bank save that of faith, so that when the flour was low in the barrel, and the meal was nearly out, the mother would go to her closet and say simply, "Lord, thou seest my need. Send help soon. Thou openest thine hand and satisfiest the desire of every living thing. Give us this day our daily bread." And that day, though the poems sent so wistfully to the far-away magazines and papers at the north often came flying back with a polite letter of rejection, there would come instead a more welcome letter with a check, and then there would be a fête day. A neighbor, anybody within four miles was a neighbor, would lend his old rockaway and his staid and quiet horse, and my friend and two or three of the children would jog to the nearest town and, as she gayly said, provision the garrison.

If the dear house-mother had been ever so rich she would still have had to do her own work, in that vicinity, for everybody else did the same, and help from outside was not to be had. Husband and children lent their willing hands, and there was no housework which the boys were ashamed or afraid to undertake, from dish washing to the harder labor of the laundry. These lads, who could iron and bake and sweep and make beds, were prepared for college by their parents, and successively went there, and were graduated with honors, paying their own way for the most part, and enduring hardness like good soldiers.

I used to receive long merry letters from this brave lady, a mother of men who fulfilled my ideal of what such a mother's boys should be; letters bright, chatty, sparkling with wit and anecdote, written by bits and snatches as she waited for the loaves in the oven to brown, or laid aside her mending for a moment's rest. She would speak of the lad at her knee reciting his Latin grammar propped up before her kneading board, or would apologize for an interrupted paragraph by explaining that Donald had just called her to come to his den and listen to his last story or ballad before he sent it away on its voyage in search of a port. "Somehow," she would add, "Donald thinks the poems have a better chance if they go off with my blessing—mine!—and I couldn't write a couplet to save my life." She could do better; she could be her husband's inspiration and his cheery comrade on the roughest road, always heartening him by her quips and sallies, always having herself the grace of going merrily onward.

A hard-working, far-reaching, useful life was

this, as the lives of good mothers must ever be. Her sons to-day represent her in many fields, they are active in countless endeavors for good; they are the unselfish, loyal and devoted husbands that such a mother could train to lift a little the burden of the great world.

To speak of the mother-brooding which enfolds the opening years of a man's life as the dearest experience which life will ever hold for him may be in a sense untrue. Man must live through multiform experiences and taste many a cup divinely brewed. There are for him sacramental days which lift him up to a plane of almost heavenly joy here and there on his progress through the world. The day when he definitely decides to stand for Christ against the temptations of lower ambition and mere temporal advantage is forever after starred for him in happiest memory.

The day when he finds his ideal enshrined in a fair woman, and she returns his love in sweet trustfulness and gracious surrender, is thenceforward a glad anniversary.

The day when the cry of the firstborn is in the house and the sweetness of heaven haloes the face of the mother is set apart as the day of the solemn feast, of the crowning and the laurel. Yet, more and more, as time goes on and youth passes, the heart of the son turns yearningly to the golden dawn when mother love made his childhood safe and sheltered and beautiful.

There is something of the woman nature in every finely tempered man, as the best women, on the other hand, have derived something from the father. Each sex complements the other in a mysterious but evident exchange of gifts, so that, were such a thing possible, a wholly feminine woman would be not altogether pleasing, and a wholly masculine man would be somewhat too arbitrary, if not too overbearing and perhaps brutal of type. In the highest style of manhood and womanhood we find the human element composed of the best in both halves of the race, so that daughters are often most like fathers, and sons most like mothers, from a law which goes deep into the primitive conditions of being. The mother who would see her sons grow up worthily must not count her life dear in the years when they are under her molding hand. She must share their pursuits from the era of balls and tops to the era of falling in love.

Never to lose her boy's confidence is the

wisest counsel which can be given a mother, but
how is she to attain this end? Only by putting
and keeping her boys first. Only by subordinat-
ing other engagements, of pleasure, of society,
of church work, of philanthropy, to the more
important appointments she has in the nursery,
on the playground and around the evening
lamp. She should know her boys' companions,
and be their friend, and partially their
confidante.

A woman whose sweet face rises in my
thought has done this for her son, though she
has been handicapped by continual literal bondage to her couch of pain during the years of his
childhood and youth. Unable to bear her
weight on the floor or to walk a single step, unable to turn herself in bed without assistance,
this woman's indomitable will has united with
her Christian courage to keep her from casting
a shadow on the wholesome sunshine of her
boy's life. She has kept pace with him in his
studies and his games, has interviewed his
teachers, stimulated him to sustained endeavor,
and given him a knowledge of what God's love
can make of woman when tried in the furnace
and seven times purified.

If a woman worn with bodily pain and spent with weakness may do so much, what may not one accomplish whose life is unfettered and who is free to go and come as she chooses?

One has only to see how quickly the ailing, sobbing baby hushes its querulous cries when taken up in the arms of a tender and loving man, its father or another, with a compassionate heart, to realize the secret of strength and gentleness combined, to get at the core of the Psalmist's meaning when he exclaims, "Thy gentleness hath made me great." Passing the love of women, passing the tenderness of women, are the love and the tenderness of men in relations which draw closely upon their reserves of sympathy. A boy who studies the needs and devotes himself to the comfort of an invalid mother will make a considerate husband to some happy woman. What the French call *petits soins* come readily to men who have had at times in their lives to look out for the welfare of somewhat dependent kinswomen.

But there is another side of the shield.

When the boys go out from the home nest to the larger world, perhaps to business, perhaps to college, the wise mother still keeps in touch with them. A good many young people in this land have heard of Hugh Beaver, that splendid fellow whose life ended on earth at twenty-four, two years ago, and who suddenly heard the Master's call to "Come up higher!" When Hugh went to college his biographer says that he was "a straight-forward, genial, sunny-hearted boy, but the more serious problems of an earnest life lay before him, and the deeper springs of his character and power were still sealed." His mother wrote to him about this time, "I hope, darling, you have learned the comfort of taking everything to God in prayer. Nothing is too trifling. Be sure to pray before leaving your room in the morning. We need our Father's help and guidance in all that we do. May the Lord bless you, and enable you to live a consistent useful life to his praise and glory, is the prayer of your loving mother."

A certain strange reluctance comes between some mothers and their sons, when matters relating to the Christian life are in concern. If we were close to our Lord would we not be able to overcome this shyness? Yet often the younger heart is waiting and longing for the word of counsel, is earnestly desiring that the older one may take the initiative in the conversation. I would that mothers should not only pray for but with their sons, kneeling beside the bed at night, drawing them now and again into their own chambers for a little tender twilight talk. We are too cowardly when we shrink from speaking of the dear Lord, and hesitate to introduce his name into our daily talk in the household.

So it happens that opportunities are lost. Souls have been almost in contact, but have glided apart. Each goes its separate way. The friend of Christ—ah me! was that friend a mother?—has been silent, and timorous, and so the Beloved has withdrawn himself and is gone. Looking at her sturdy little man, mother may feel like saying:

"My laddie, O my laddie, I am wistful as I clasp
  Your little hand within my own, and think how many men
    Gone far from earth and memory, beyond our mortal grasp,
  Are living and are breathing, dear child, in you again.

"My laddie of the golden hair, there stand at God's right hand
  His saints who went through blood and flame, the yeomen of our line;

And there are seraphs singing in the glorious better
    land
  Whose heart-beats kept, when here on earth, the
      pace of yours and mine.

"Kneel, little laddie, at my side; there's no defense
    like this,
  An evening prayer in childish trust, and let him
    scoff who may;
A daily prayer to God above, a gentle mother's kiss,
  Will keep my little laddie safe, however dark the
      day."

"What shall I do about taking my restless boys to church?" asked a mother of a dear aged minister who had been her girlhood's pastor. "They do not understand the services, and find them tedious; they fidget and complain of Sunday as a wearisome day. Would I not do better to postpone their church-going until they are older?"

"No," was the reply. "Train them up in the way they should go. By accustoming them to constant attendance in God's house, you will form in them a good habit." We are unfortunately bringing up a generation which does not feel the obligation of keeping holy the Lord's Day, which acts its own pleasure, not seeks to know God's will in this matter. Mothers must look to this and reform it.

Indeed they can. And here let me add that good behavior in church is just as important as good behavior anywhere else, and part of it begins at the very beginning; in being in church a little while before the service commences. In our home in my childhood, at family worship, my father had a way, which I remember pleasantly in contrast with the hurrying methods of to-day, of starting everything with a margin, so that nobody should be late. He insisted that the young people of the house should always come to prayers if they were well, and he himself, Bible in hand, would be seated five minutes before the appointed time, waiting for us all to come. I can see him now across the years, his gray hair brushed back from his serene face, his eyes lighted with a rare inner smile, his look expressing the greatest patience.

"I like to compose my mind," he would say, "before I enter the presence of the King."

I can hear him softly crooning his favorite hymn, if I lean back in my chair and listen— hear it as if the voice which sung these stanzas had not been for many long years singing with the Redeemer above. And his voice was very sweet as he sang:

"How happy are they
Who the Saviour obey,
And have laid up their treasure above.
O what tongue can express
The sweet comfort and peace
Of a soul in its earliest love."

One of the unwritten laws always observed in this good man's home was that nobody should be tardy to church. This habit clings to me still. I am distressed and humiliated if ever by accident I am so late that I must walk down the aisle after the pastor has begun the service. It seems to me as impolite to be late at church as to be late at any other function which has a fixed hour for starting.

Besides, it is really unnecessary. The habitually tardy person usually catches his train, if this is important in his day's engagements, and the train labeled, "Divine service, half-past ten o'clock," can be as easily caught if one chooses to take pains in the matter.

I hold that the thoroughly well-bred person will be well behaved in church. He or she will sit still. He will not whisper, she will not giggle, neither will comment on the people who have come to church, neither will make secular engagements while service is going on. Above all things no decently behaved person will read printed calendars, or turn over leaflets, or pull letters from his pocket, or fumble through the hymn-book, while the Commandments or the Scripture lessons are being read. I have seen well-dressed and intelligent people doing these things, and they were convicted of impoliteness and lack of training by their actions.

Crowning impropriety of all, no one with any claim to good breeding will pull out a watch and consult it during the service.

I observe that many persons coming late into church drop their heads upon their pews for their private devotions with no reference to what is going on at the moment. This does not seem to me quite right. A better way is to unite in whatever part of the service is in progress; one's own little prayer being supposed to anticipate the entire worship, not to interject itself on the worship which is appointed. As the old Psalm has it, we may declare:

> "I joyed when to the house of God
> Go up, they said to me.
> Jerusalem, within thy gates
> Our feet shall standing be."

"If I forget thee, O Jerusalem, let my right hand forget her cunning." "I would rather be a doorkeeper in the house of my God than to dwell in the tents of wickedness."

This is the heart's cry of the generation which are brought up to serve the King in his sacred courts.

In the intercourse of families there is often too little demonstration. Affection should freely express itself. We are much too apt to take for granted the fact that we love one another. In the truly well-regulated Christian household there is little need for discipline as expressed in punishment. Coercion is unheard of. A habit of referring everything to the arbitration of the Heavenly Father keeps disobedience to the earthly parents far from the happy fold. The mother should not exact of her boys submission to her authority because she intimates a wish; she stands to them as one who is carrying out the will of God, and who desires to help them to understand and obey the same sweet will. There can be no jars in a home attuned to the Divine harmonies. Let the mother dwell with God and her children will be brought into God's Kingdom.

"I saw the Holy Spirit shining in my mother's face through all my boyhood," said a college professor, "and her piety and faithfulness drew us, a large family, safe into the service of the Master, though our father was not a Christian until we were all grown up."

A mother should be satisfied for her children with no development but the best, and the best is not found outside of that company in which Jesus is the chief and the dearest guest.

> "In the secret of his presence
>   From the hurrying world I hide,
> In the secret of his presence
>   Very safely I abide.
> *And he gives me many a sign*
>   *Of his grace and love divine.*
>
> "Care and labor are my portion,
>   Toil and care till evensong,
> But the hours, though often weary,
>   Never drag their load along.
> For the blessing of the Master
>   Makes the heaviest burden light,
> In the secret of his presence
>   When I dwell from morn till night.
>
> "In the secret of his presence
>   Any cross he bids me take,
> Garlanded with sweetest flowers,
>   Wears the legend 'For his sake.'
> I am happy as I serve him,
>   Happy as I walk the road
> Which my Master went before me,
>   Straight unto the throne of God.
> *For he gives me many a sign*
>   *Of his grace and power divine.*"

CHAPTER XIII

Linked with Many Lives

The recluse shuts himself in his study, finds delight in his books or his musings and shuns society. He may do no man wrong, he may even do good after a fashion of his own, but he lives a self-centered and self-absorbed life. It is better that one should touch others at many points, that one should be interested in his fellows, that more and more one should seek to know and to care for persons outside of his own immediate circle, and to observe life and affairs from a viewpoint that is not wholly one's own.

At an early age the threads of contact with other homes begin to weave themselves into the woof of our being. First the kindred are our only associates, the father, mother, grandfather and grandmother, brothers, sisters, uncles, aunts, cousins. The family feeling strikes deep roots; we care for those of our own blood, we belong to them, and they to us. But with school days we begin to form our friendships beyond the threshold of the home. There is a

little golden-haired girl who sits beside us in the
class, there is a shock-headed boy who walks
home from school with us, and we learn through
intercourse with them that there are people
worth knowing in the world besides those who
live at our house. I sat beside a child's desk
this summer in a little red schoolhouse in the
mountains and Whittier's lines came back
to me:

> "Still sits the schoolhouse by the road,
>   A ragged beggar sleeping;
> Around it still the sumachs grow
>   And blackberry vines are creeping.
>
> "Within, the master's desk is seen
>   Deep scarred by raps official,
> The warping floor, the battered seats,
>   The jackknife's carved initial.
>
> "The charcoal frescoes on its wall,
>   Its door's worn sill, betraying
> The feet that, creeping slow to school,
>   Went storming out to playing!
>
> "Long years ago a winter sun
>   Shone over it at setting;
> Lit up its western window panes
>   And low eaves' icy-fretting.
>
> "It touched the tangled golden curls
>   And brown eyes, full of grieving,
> Of one who still her steps delayed
>   When all the school were leaving.

"For near her stood the little boy
  Her childish favor singled;
His cap pulled low upon a face
  Where pride and shame were mingled.

"Pushing with restless feet the snow
  To right and left he lingered;
As restlessly her tiny hands
  The blue checked apron fingered.

"He saw her lift her eyes; he felt
  The soft hand's light caressing,
And heard the tremble of her voice
  As if a fault confessing.

" 'I'm sorry that I spelt the word;
  I hate to go above you,
Because,' the brown eyes lower fell,
  'Because, you see, I love you.'

"Still memory to a gray-haired man
  That sweet child-face is showing;
Dear girl, the grasses o'er her grave
  Have forty years been growing.

"He lives to learn in life's hard school
  How few who pass above him
Lament their triumph and his loss
  Because, like her, they love him."

Some of my happiest recollections are of my
school days when I was a rosy romping child
drawn to school over the snow on a playmate's
sled. The red apples and doughnuts which
we shared at luncheon had a toothsome flavor

unsurpassed by any delicate viands of later years. As a child of ten, in a school on the banks of the Passaic conducted by three lovely sisters who have gone to their rest, leaving behind them the record of a fruitful life full of faithful work for the Master, I formed some of life's most lasting friendships. Still, in our autumn, women who were girls with me in the sweet spring of our days come to sit beside my fire, and to talk over the lessons we were taught by Miss Anna and Miss Elizabeth Rogers. Our beautiful sainted Miss Jane went very early to the other land, ere her youth had faded, and while her cheek was round and her dark eyes bright with the light of love and joy.

From those dear teachers I first learned that life cannot be lived alone, that each life must link itself with many others. We are partakers of that Divine nature which gathers to its breast and bears upon its everlasting arms the successive generations of our race. In God's heart there is room for all. Our Saviour in his wonderful prayer before he left the world included his own who should believe in him to every age, and the sweet meaning comforts us in all tribulation; the tender fullness of that prayer makes glad our waste places, and feeds our soul hunger. Reverently may we in one respect compare ourselves with God, for, made in his image, he has not habited us in mean raiment, or compelled us to dwell in cramped quarters. Our souls live in palaces many-chambered, and fair, and in one room we receive some of our guests, and in another we welcome others, and there are beautiful withdrawing rooms where we hold converse with our very dearest dear.

We need not be afraid of making new friendships. Love in its supremest royalty comes not to everyone. There are beautiful natures which, for one reason or another, dwell in singleness throughout their pilgrimage, but these are very often most generously endowed with a capacity for making and keeping friends.

Besides, in the changes of the swiftly moving years, the landscape of our lives is always subject to alteration.

> "Friend after friend departs,
> Who hath not lost a friend?
> There is no union here of hearts
> That finds not here an end."

We must keep adding to our stock of friends, must be responsive to new claimants, must keep open doors for the good and the true. How delightful it is to think not only of all the pleasant people we have met but of the unknown visitants whom we are yet to meet. We never go to an unfamiliar town, to a mountain or seaside hostelry, to a little hamlet high up and hidden away in the hills, that we do not discover somebody who on one side of our nature attracts us; somebody whom we can bless by our giving or from whom we can take a blessing.

We retain our youth by our susceptibility to friendship. He who has lost desire to win and pleasure in keeping friends has gone far into the shadowy realm of old age. Selfishness may breed a premature decrepitude of the affections. We must be careful not to lose interest in our neighbors, not to become indifferent to acquaintances—new or of longer standing.

Our lives may go out into all the earth if we are coworkers in the great missionary movements for evangelizing the world. Away off in New Mexico, many miles from kith and kin, in a community where none but themselves speak English, two brave girls are teaching little children the way of life, and showing to those around them the light of a Christian home. God bless our fearless home missionaries, working steadfastly for him in dark corners where they face peril, loneliness and discouragement. Out in Dakota, in a sod house, dwell a missionary family, father, mother, children, in poverty and privation, fighting for the Master, and making a center for his disciples to gather around him. Shall we not care for these—not merely by sending a box or a barrel, now and then, filled with needed clothing and household supplies—by our prayers, our thoughts, our love?

Far over the ocean, in Northern India, in China, in Japan, in the Islands under our flag, there are heroic men and women toiling "In His Name." Our beloved foreign missionaries are too often forgotten when they are off, beyond our sight and hearing, in the remoteness of their exile.

"The greatest hardship the missionary has to bear," says Dr. R. B. Peary, "is his loneliness and isolation. Separated almost entirely from his own race, he is deprived of all those social joys that are so dear to him. The thought of his kinsmen and friends is ever in his mind, but, alas! they are so far away. He must go on, year after year, living among a people from whom an impassable gulf separates him, leading the same lonely life. For the first year or two he rather enjoys the quiet and privacy, but by and by it becomes almost unendurable."

Dr. Edmund Lawrence, on the same subject thus sums up the whole matter, "Very many of the missionary's heaviest burdens are included in the one word, whose height and breadth and length and depth none knows so well as he—the word 'exile.' It is not merely a physical exile from home and country and all their interests; it is not only an intellectual exile from all that would feed and stimulate the mind; it is yet more, a spiritual exile from the guidance, the instruction, the support, the fellowship and the communion of the church at home."

Furthermore, after a few years of absence, the missionary hears seldom from the home land, except as official communications come from the boards of the church, or epistles arrive from his immediate family. "Even these latter become less and less frequent. The arrival of the mails, which at first was looked forward to with so much joy, is now scarcely noted. 'After a few years of residence in the East one feels that he is largely out of touch with the life of the West, and that he is forgotten by home and friends."

Here may some of us not discover a mission? May we not devote some part of our time to the sending of good cheer to our foreign missionaries? Not writing them perfunctory letters, nor filling those we do send with exclusively religious news, but giving them glimpses of our life at home, of our books, our music, our pictures, and our household gayeties. Even our new bonnets may interest a missionary woman living where nobody wears a bonnet.

The main thing is to remember that no man liveth to himself and no man dieth to himself; that we are bound in one bundle, and must bear one another's burdens, and, if we would be Christ-like, must keep in touch with many lives.

Shall I show you a leaf, now, from the daily life of a home missionary?

The wind whistled and the snow sifted into every crevice of the log cabin in which Mr. and Mrs. Harmstead and their children had made their home for the last six months. They had carefully stuffed every aperture with rags and

paper, and covered the walls with pictures cut
from the old numbers of *Harper's Weekly* and
other periodicals which found their way to this
little Western home. Still, there were nooks
and crannies which neither wife nor husband
could make so weathertight that they were
proof against the wild storms of the region. A
year ago their home had been more comfortable,
but in a fierce cyclone, months before, the little
frame house had been blown down, and the only
place in which the missionary and his wife could
find shelter was this little log cabin, originally
built by a settler who had in time abandoned it
for more comfortable quarters. The church
next door was really a better refuge against
winter storms than the house in which the minister had his dwelling. Indeed, there were occasions when Mrs. Harmstead was compelled to
hurry her brood out of the cabin and into the
church that they might sleep in some degree of
warmth and comfort. The benches on which
the children sat at the table belonged to the
church, and were carried in there for services
on Sundays, and on week days when the people
came to prayer meeting.

This morning it seemed to the Harmsteads

that it would be safer to move over into the church till the weather changed. So, taking a few necessary cooking utensils and what bedding they could carry, the family migrated, fearing that the storm would make it impossible for them to do so later in the day. The church could at least be made comfortable.

Once settled there, Mr. Harmstead seated himself in a corner to study his sermon for the next day, while his wife established the children with their books and toys, and herself read for the twentieth time a letter which had reached her a day or two previous.

The letter was from the ladies of the church at home to which she had belonged in her girlhood. When Emily Fuller married Duncan Harmstead there was no prettier girl or fairer bride in all the township and surrounding country. A college graduate, she was familiar with the best that books and art could give her, and her home had been replete with every refinement and the comforts which people in ordinary circumstances in the East enjoy as a matter of course. Going with her husband to his field of service in Nebraska, the young wife understood that she was accepting hardness, and that self-denial and privation would to some extent be her portion. The years, seven, since her marriage day, had flown rapidly along, but they had done the work of fourteen on the sweet face of the woman who had shared poverty, labor, and many a grief at her husband's side, always uncomplainingly, though the many cares had left their mark upon her nature. She was less hopeful now than once, and sometimes her buoyant faith failed her for a little time. It sometimes seemed as if God had forgotten her. Often she said to herself, "If my dear ones at home realized the daily suffering of a missionary's lot, surely they would do something to lighten it." By a series of circumstances not unusual in families, those nearest of kin to her had either died or become so impoverished that they could give her little substantial help, and Mr. Harmstead was a man with few relatives on whom to call. The salary of a home missionary is small at best. In the case of Mr. Harmstead it was seldom fully paid and never promptly. The Board sent some aid to the struggling Western church, but there was always a great discrepancy between income and outgo on the part of both the missionary and the church. The letter read as follows. Mrs. Harmstead knew it by heart:

"DEAR EMILY: Your old friends in Hazleton Church wish to send you a present which will be just what you want. Now, with the utmost frankness, will you let us know what to pack in the barrel or barrels which we are sending to your far-away home. Do not fail to tell us just what you and the good man and the bairns are most in want of, and so far as we can we will try to meet your needs. We consider this a privilege, and are only sorry that it did not sooner occur to us that for *our* missionary we might take one dear lady who grew up among us and whom we fondly remember."

The letter had touched a very tender chord in Mrs. Harmstead's heart, and as she sat down to answer it she was divided between the wish to state exactly her needs and a little feeling of delicacy in revealing the extent of her poverty. She decided at last that candor was the only course; that as God had opened this door for her it was her place to walk through it, not thinking about the impression she would make on her old friends, but merely telling the exact truth. So taking her pad and pencil, for the minister was using the only inkstand and the only pen they possessed, she said:

"Dear Friends: I have hesitated a little how to answer your kindest of letters, but I have resolved at last that the only thing for me to do is to be entirely truthful. We are literally in need of everything. My husband is destitute of underclothing (on another slip of paper I give you his size). He has no overcoat and this weather is freezing. Last winter he wore all the year only a mackintosh, which is now threadbare, and an old shawl of mine wound around his shoulders in the coldest days. Neither my husband nor any of the children have decent stockings or shoes (on another slip of paper I give you the sizes). Little Bertha has outgrown all her frocks, and I have made them over for Ruth. Eddie is in rags and tatters; not one of the children is decently clad or even comfortably. I say nothing about myself; but I have not had a new gown other than a calico since my marriage, seven years ago, nor have I had a new pair of gloves since that time —a pair of mittens would be a luxury. However, it makes very little difference about me; I can stay in the house, but I do long to have

something warm for my husband and something
to keep the children from cold and chilblains
in this fearfully bitter climate. We do not
suffer for lack of food, as our people are very
kind, and thus far the Lord has always sent us
supplies as he did Elijah by the brook Cherith;
but we never have ready money, and when our
money does come we have to pay it all out at the
store in return for bills that have accrued. I
am not sorry that I came with my husband to
this hard field. God has sent us here, and he
is enabling us to light a candle in a dark place.
I have no regrets or repinings. We have been
very happy in each other and with our dear children; but there come days when we would like
to be in touch with our old friends. If you can
slip a new book or two into the barrel for my
husband it would be an unspeakable boon. He
would enjoy Edersheim's *Life of Christ* so much
that I mention it, and that book does not cost
very much now, as I see by a paper which comes
from some kind friend's hand every week. As
I read over what I have written I fear you will
think me lacking in delicacy, for I simply have
put in such a revelation of our poverty as you
will hardly believe can exist. So, dear friends,

pack in the barrel what you please, confident that very little can come amiss in our house, and do not forget to pray for your old friend and for the work of God in this distant place. Pray for a blessing on my husband's parish.

"Affectionately yours,

"EMILY HARMSTEAD."

A passing teamster took the letter that day to the post office, and in due time it found its way to the Sewing Society in the church which had been Emily Fuller's old home. The ladies were seated in the comfortable church parlor. They were all warmly and beautifully dressed. A sweet-faced woman presided at a table and gave out rolls of garments to the needlewomen; the flow of talk, with intermittent peals of soft laughter, went smoothly on; there was a pleasant air of friendship about the circle. After a while the president rapped on the table for silence and said, "I have a letter to read to you from our old friend, Mrs. Harmstead, who is, as most of you know, a home missionary in Nebraska. Some weeks ago I wrote asking for just the account she gives of what may be needed there, and now I will read us the letter."

The Sewing Meeting.

As she did so a hush fell upon the group. One by one put down her sewing and tears came to eyes which were suddenly blurred. When the letter was finished there was a little spell of quiet, broken by the minister's wife, who said, "Let us pray." Kneeling in her place, she offered a heartfelt prayer for the far-away sister whom they had forgotten and for the work of God which this sister and her husband were carrying on so handicapped. She prayed God, too, to forgive their own neglect and hardness of heart.

After that, you may be sure, it was not long before contributions came pouring in for the barrels, which were presently packed and on their way to the Harmsteads. It is little to say that every need was supplied. There was a new gown of warm cashmere for Mrs. Harmstead, in the pocket of which was a purse containing a little roll of bills. The minister found in his overcoat a pocketbook also lined pleasantly with money. Everything which the children could require was lovingly inserted here and there in the wonderful barrels, and, best of all, the ladies of the church decided that the thing they would next do would be to raise money to erect a snug parsonage for this minister's family, so that it might not face another Western winter unprotected against the elements.

When the barrels arrived you may be sure there was a deep thanksgiving in the house of the home missionary. A thanksgiving which lasted a long time.

CHAPTER XIV

The Keeping of Home Anniversaries

Our American tendency is to diminish the importance of recreation and to set too high a value on work. We are usually obliged to work strenuously, and, far from being a misfortune, this is a blessing, strengthening and toughening character and bracing whatever is best in our mental and moral natures. But play has its uses too, and demonstration, which retires to the background when we are working at high pressure, comes to the front when we take a holiday.

Birthdays afford an opportunity for family festivity which should not be overlooked. Mother's birthday, father's birthday, the birthday of each son and daughter should be observed in some pleasant fashion—with personal greetings and gifts, with the coming in of friends. Each year, as we enter it, should be marked with a white stone; it is a stage in our progress; it affords us a chance to turn over a new leaf in our life's volume.

The years, slow-footed in childhood, race rapidly onward when we reach the later seasons of our career. There come over us shadows and clouds of depression sometimes as we think how fast they go and how little we have accomplished. With the poet we exclaim sorrowfully, on some gray November day when the frost is on the stubble and the trees are shivering:

> "We too have autumns when our leaves
>   Drop loosely through the dampened air;
> When all our good seems bound in sheaves
>   And we stand reaped and bare."

Such moods should not be encouraged. They rob us of strength, though their tender melancholy is very attractive.

Better far is that temper of mind which I remember in my honored father, cheery from youth to age, and singing about the house, with a spirit which care could never daunt nor dim in its radiant brightness. One of his favorite hymns was that dear old lyric of Charles Wesley, with its lilt of the lark uprising in the morning:

> "Come, let us anew our journey pursue,
>   Roll round with the year
> And never stand still till the Master appear.

His adorable will let us gladly fulfill,
   And our talent improve
By the patience of hope and the labor of love."

And another favorite was the hymn in the same peculiar, and at one time popular, measure, containing these stanzas:

"Of heavenly birth, though wandering on earth
   This is not our place;
But strangers and pilgrims ourselves we confess.

"At Jesus's call we gave up our all;
   And still we forego,
For Jesus's sake, our enjoyments below.
No longing we find for the country behind,
   But onward we move,
And still we are seeking a country above:

"A country of joy without any alloy;
   We thither repair;
Our hearts and our treasure already are there.

   *   *   *   *   *

"The rougher our way the shorter our stay;
   The tempests that rise
Shall gloriously hurry our souls to the skies.
The fiercer the blast the sooner 'tis past;
   The troubles that come
Shall come to our rescue, and hasten us home."

The dominant note of our Christian life should be that of rejoicing. Lifted above anxiety, set free from solicitudes and from irritations, we should take time to be happy. Every holiday, whether peculiar to our own home or set in the annual calendar, should arrive on our threshold as if it were an angel visitant, and therefore welcome.

Anniversaries often emphasize the absence of dear ones. Our beloved son is in the distant East, keeping Christmas as best he can to the sound of the drum beat and the bugle call in a country which has no reminder of home except the flag under which he serves. But we can pray for him and he need not be left out of the joy, though in visible presence he cannot now share it. It is for the mother whose laddie is out of her sight to be brave and patient in this time of trial which has come to the great republic.

For such a mother I have written:

CHRISTMAS FAR AFIELD

Shut your eyes, mother darling, now shut your eyes
    and sleep,
The wind is like a wolf outside, yet do not wake and
    weep;
For overhead the stars are bright, and O! I see one
    Star
I'm sure can shine on Willie, it sends its light so far;
Our Willie leal and loving, and in the alien land
The one they need to set things right, so brave of heart
    and hand;

A lonesome time without him, yes, and little Christ-
    mas joy
For a mother white and grieving, and hungry for her
    boy.
But the country is a mother too, and sent her son
    away,
And that's why some of us are sad this merry Christ-
    mas Day.
Yet God is here, and God is there, and duty must be
    done,
And not a mother of us all would dare withhold her
    son
When the wooing bugles called him, and the throbbing
    drums said "come,"
And he carried o'er the ocean the conscience of his
    home.

Shut your eyes, little mother, shut your eyes and sleep.
'Tis Christmas Eve, and o'er the fields the snow is
    drifting deep,
The air is full of music, it is thrilling sweet and far,
There's naught to hinder angels, who fly from star to
    star,
From singing o'er that tropic camp as once they sang
    of old,
When they leaned so low from heaven, o'er tender
    lambs in fold;
And Willie pacing up and down, upon his sentry's
    beat
May hear the seraph melodies, so wonderful and fleet;
I'm told those Eastern places have a magic not like
    ours,
And spells and dreams that linger there, with curious
    mystic powers;
You may cease from fretting, mother; the Christmas
    joy will be
Undimmed and beautiful about our lad beyond the sea.

Why, mother dear, the fretting, 'tis for them that stay
    behind
And hear the music die away to silence on the wind;
And it's always glory beckoning the happy ones who go,
And who'll come back some splendid day triumphant
    o'er the foe;
Then what a Christmas-keeping, from the prairies to
    the lakes,
From the pine-lands to the palm-lands, where'er old
    ocean breaks
In surf and thunder on our coasts, what Christmas-
    keeping *then*,
When Columbia calls her soldiers back; great mother
    of strong men!

Now, shut your eyes, sweet mother, just shut your
    eyes and sleep,
No doubt the mother of the Christ her thoughtful
    watch would keep
When she saw him going from her and she could not
    do a thing—
Nor take much comfort from that hour when she
    heard the angels sing.
Perhaps she never heard them, on that night when he
    was born,
And she lay all wan and tired, in the faint and roseate
    morn;
But, born to be a Saviour, that was all the joy she
    knew;
And, in a lesser way of course, such joy may come to
    you.
For, not for self, and not for pelf, but at the country's
    need,
Our Willie went, at duty's call, to do, to dare, to heed,
And, wherever floats the flag to-day, and far as he may
    roam,
He carries with him, mother dear, the conscience of
    his home.

When the new year knocks at the door it is well for us to remember some of the old words which have ever been the consolations and delights of the saints: "Lord, thou hast been our dwelling place in all generations." "The Lord shall preserve thy going out and thy coming in." "I, the Lord, have called thee in righteousness, and will hold thine hand, and will keep thee." "Thou wilt keep him in perfect peace whose mind is stayed on thee, because he trusteth in thee."

> "Workman of God! O! lose not heart,
>   But learn what God is like,
> And in the darkest battle field
>   Thou shalt know where to strike."

The daily routine of the household apparently so tranquil has its pitfalls, its conflicts, and its temptations. To keep one's voice sweet, one's face bright, one's will steady, one's patience unperturbed, in the arena of the home, in the presence of one's own family, is no light task. Home joy is a precious thing and should be guarded.

> "If I had known in the morning
>   How wearily all the day
> The words unkind would trouble my mind,
>   I said, when you went away,

I had been more careful, darling,
  Nor given you needless pain;
But we vex our own with look and tone
  We might never take back again.

"For though in the quiet evening
  You should give me the kiss of peace,
Yet it well might be that never for me
  The pain of the heart should cease.
How many go forth at morning
  Who never come home at night;
And hearts have broken for harsh words spoken
  That sorrow can ne'er set right.

"We have careful thought for the stranger,
  And smiles for the sometime guest;
But yet for our own the bitter tone,
  Though we love our own the best;
Ah, lip with the curve impatient,
  Ah, brow with the look of scorn,
'Twere a cruel fate were the night too late
  To undo the work of morn."

Away back in A. D. 700 one of God's dear children wrote this little prayer, which is appropriate for working days and holidays alike:

"Grant us, O Lord, to pass this day in gladness and peace, without stumbling and without stain; that, reaching the eventide victorious over all temptation, we may praise thee, the eternal God, who art blessed, and dost govern all things, world without end. Amen."

The wedding anniversaries are very precious in the happy home. I was a privileged guest

recently at the fortieth wedding day of a dear
friend to whom God had given nine dear children and in whose circle there is not yet one
vacant chair.   Many of the guests at the wedding dinner had been present at the bridal,
and they exchanged reminiscences and renewed
felicitations.   The merriment was unclouded,
and it was hallowed by the felt and recognized
presence of the Master at the feast.

CHAPTER XV

THE PLANT HEART'S-EASE

WHEN one sees the serene faces the Friends carry under their dove colored poke bonnets, and observes how noble and dignified is the writing of time on those gentle brows, one is aware that in their bosoms they have been carrying the plant heart's-ease. This little herb grows not in the soil of pride and flourishes not amid arrogance and contempt. Bunyan tells us that it is oftenest found in the Valley of Humiliation. "It is fat ground" there, he says, "and, as you see, consisteth much in meadows; and if a man were to come here in the summer time, as we do now, if he knew not anything before thereof, and if he also delighted himself in the sight of his eyes, he might see that that would be delightful to him. Behold, how green this valley is! also how beautified with lilies! I have also known many laboring men that have got good estates in this Valley of Humiliation (for God resisteth the proud, but gives more, more grace to the humble); for indeed it is a very fruitful soil, and doth bring forth by handfuls. Some also have wished that the next way to their Father's house were here, that they might be troubled no more with either hills or mountains to go over; but the way is the way, and there's an end."

"Now," goes on the poet dreamer, "as they were going along and talking, they espied a boy feeding his father's sheep. The boy was in very mean clothes, but of a very fresh and well favored countenance; and as he sat by himself, he sung." And these were the words:

> "He that is down needs fear no fall,
>   He that is low no pride;
> He that is humble ever shall
>   Have God to be his guide.
> I am content with what I have,
>   Little be it or much;
> And, Lord, contentment still I crave,
>   Because thou savest such.
> Fullness to such a burden is
>   As go on pilgrimage:
> Here little, and hereafter bliss,
>   Is best from age to age."

"I will dare to say," said Greatheart, "that this boy lives a merrier life, and wears more of that herb called heart's-ease in his bosom, than he that is clad in silk and velvet."

To have the perfume of the plant heart's-ease

about one all the while one must cultivate a spirit of trust. She who doubts God and his continual loving kindness will have no heart's-ease. She who is careful and troubled about health, about money, about the morrow, either for herself or for her loved ones, will never have peace for her comrade. She who is straining to keep up appearances, unwilling to live plainly, to dress plainly, to take an inconspicuous seat at the banquet, will not get away from care.

Then, too, she who carries her loads for herself, or for her home people and her business associates, to the cross, *and carries the loads away again,* will not know the balm of heart's-ease. Whoever kneels to the Lord in contrite prayer, and accepts the promises literally, will bear ease about with him, wherever he may walk, whatever he may do or bear.

William Law, mystic and preacher of the gospel more than a hundred years ago, living in Putney, England, found out the secret of heart's-ease. "When things seemed to go ill with the cause of truth and righteousness, in controversy or in actual life, Law fell back at once on the assurance that God's ways must be a great deep to the mind of man. And when hurts and wrongs, crosses and vexations, came to himself Law knew himself well enough to see why God sent them or permitted them to come. 'You are here,' he said to himself, 'to have no tempers and no self-designs, and no self-ends, but to fill some place and act some part in strict conformity and thankful resignation to the divine pleasure. Begin, therefore, in the smallest matters and most ordinary occasions 'and accustom your mind to the daily exercise of this pious temper in the lowest occurrences of life. And when a contempt, an affront, a little injury, a loss or a disappointment, or the smallest events in every day continually raise your mind to God in proper acts of resignation, then you may justly hope that you shall be numbered among those who are resigned and thankful to God in the greatest trials and afflictions.' "

Said Geo. Klingle:

"God broke our years to hours and days that
    Hour by hour,
    And day by day,
Just going on a little way,
We might be able all along
    To keep quite strong.

Should all the weight of life
Be laid across our shoulders, and the future, **rife**
With woe and struggle, meet us face to face
At just one place,
We could not go;
Our feet would stop; and so
God lays a little on us every day,
And never, I believe, on all the way
Will burdens bear so deep
Or pathways lie so steep
But we can go if, by God's power,
We only bear the burden of the hour."

How shall we carry heart's-ease to the bereaved? How except by expressing our sympathy? "I never know just what to say to people who are in sorrow so I never say anything, if I can help it. And the more I feel the less I can say. I can write a note of condolence quite easily, for the stilted phrases slip easily from the pen, even when I know that they are useless, for they never comfort the least bit. But when I am face to face with bereavement I am dumb, although my heart may ache. Still, it makes little difference; words don't help people in grief. And, if they did, all I could say would be, 'I am sorry.'"

As if that were not the best thing to say! That simple phrase carries with it more true sympathy than dozens of stilted expressions.

When we were in sorrow and felt as if we were numbed by the awful loneliness of our grief, that seemed ours and ours only, what did it mean to us when our friend came, and putting her arms about us, sobbed, "O, my dear, I am so sorry! so sorry!" That genuine, unpremeditated outburst brought sympathy that softened grief, although nothing could lessen it. It is a mistake to think that so-called letters of condolence do no good. Of course they cannot relieve sorrow, but to the grief-stricken there is great comfort in knowing that somebody cares; that the thoughts and prayers of friends are with her who walks in the Valley of the Shadow of Death. And to one in sorrow the world in general seems such a heartless, careless place!

Let us not feel that, because dozens of other people have written letters or spoken phrases of pity to the bereaved friend, our little note or word is unnecessary. It may be just the touch of sympathy that will soften the rebellious grief and bring much-needed tears; it may be just the drop of sweet in the cup of bitterness that, but for that tiny drop, would be intolerable.

A thoughtful writer has bidden us "cultivate the undergrowth of little pleasures." She says:

"There are the things that can be done in odd minutes. They need not necessarily be simply profitable. It is highly edifying to know how some people have improved their minds in fragments of time, but to an overworked mortal what a weariness it is! Momentary snatches of good times are not a purposeless waste. Life's larger deeds and duties are usually hyphenated by some little thing. Let the in-betweens be pleasant, if possible.

"A busy housewife, on mending day, took a choice book to the sewing-room, and after slipping the needle in and out of the yawning hole in a stocking a certain number of times she read a delightful page of the story. Her work was foremost, and was duly finished, while a page at a time was not much of the book, but she made the most of the little undergrowth of pleasure and found it refreshing.

"If it is possible to manage between times the brief informal visit, or bit of neighborliness, where one cannot take a day for social interchange nor put one's self in array for a grand function, cultivate the *undergrowth of sociability*. If a favorite accomplishment must be relegated to chinks and corners of time, so be it, but let it fill the chinks. Touch the piano keys in the twilight, or redeem a season somehow for taking up the brush, or the small implements of fancy work, if that is a pleasure. Keep the pen within reach, and let the giving and taking of pleasure in a friendly letter be a common thing, not a formidable task like the writing of a state paper. Your friends can find state papers in the public library. They want to know your common goings and comings, and what you are thinking about, what you are reading and what you are making, how your new frock looks, and how the last recipe you tried came out. They want to know of your remembrance and regard, and the impulsive rhetoric of the heart is better for telling this than any studied eloquence. Those who do not cultivate this undergrowth of little pleasures in friendly letters, after the fashion of Cowper's ideal, who 'loved talking letters dearly,' do not know what they miss. There is such refreshment in the writing and the receiving that one sometimes feels moved to repeat the assertion that

'The very dearest and sweetest thing
Is the sound in the house of the postman's ring.'

"Under the severely useful and profitable crop of commonplace deeds and duties, as indistinguishable from each other, perhaps, as crowding cornstalks or swaying wheatblades, there is an undergrowth of innocent satisfaction in the ability to do the work, the growing facility in it, and in the mere fact of accomplishing it. Take the good of this comfortable feeling as you go along. Even under distasteful toils pleasant little things grow up, and a little sprig of content, planted, watered, cultivated sincerely, will blossom into pleasure by and by."

Rev. Dr. C. H. Parkhurst tells us that

"We should show ourselves neither philosophic nor Christian by declining to enjoy a landscape that is beauteous in summer on the ground that it is certain to become bleak in winter. You can bless God for the flower that blossoms at the roadside in June although you may know that no flower will be there next December. Indeed, by affecting to make light of the uncertain mercies that come to us and stay but a little while, we are certain to put ourselves a little farther beyond the reach of mercies that may come to us and stay a great while and always. One of the saddest things that parents ever say about a child that God has loaned them only a few years and then taken back is that they are afraid that God did it to punish them for having loved the child so passionately; as though any gift—most of all such a gift—if only cherished with a heart that is at the same time mindful of the blessed Author of the gift could have any other effect than to make real and dear the unseen world out of which it is come and the unseen hand by whom it was bestowed."

After all, he has the most of that sweet plant called heart's-ease who has most of tender communion with the Master. To lean on the bosom of Jesus is to know the sweetness of his grace; to hear him say in the dusk and in the dew, in the starlight and in the sunlight, "I have called you friend."

Then may we say:

"I can never doubt his goodness;
  I must ever trust his love.
By a cord that cannot sever
  I am bound to my home above.

"Henceforward on my journey
  I therefore walk by faith,
Till he give me fuller vision
  On the other side of death."

CHAPTER XVI

THE EASTER JOY

A GOLDEN WAY

FROM Christmas unto Easter
  There leads a golden way;
By solemn stars 'tis lighted,
  By angels watched each day.

We who have heard the Master
  Say, "Rise, and follow me,"
Are swift the silver milestones
  Of that dear way to see.

We walk again with Jesus
  Through those first hidden years
Ere yet he knew the anguish
  Of struggle, toil and tears.

We tread the steep hill passes,
  We stand beside the wave,
And o'er us is the blessing
  Of him who came to save.

By beds of pain we meet him;
  He gives the blind their sight;
In lonely mountain places
  He tarries oft by night.

And ever where he wanders,
  In shadow or in sun,
We catch a gleam of glory
  From God's most holy One.

"Last at the Cross, and Earliest at the Tomb."

And when they cry "Hosanna,"
  Or "Crucify" they cry,
Alike he wears the beauty
  Of God's own Son most high.

For, swift he came from heaven
  With sinful men to dwell,
And sweetest name he weareth
  Is aye "Immanuel!"

No grave could keep him captive,
  Nor death could hold him fast;
All whom he saves shall with him
  Inherit life at last.

By solemn stars love-lighted,
  By angels watched each day,
From Christmas unto Easter
  Is just one golden way.

One day at noon during the latter part of
Lent, in a cold winter, I found myself in the
neighborhood of a church on Broadway, New
York, where through open doors a stream of
people was passing in to a little service. The
invitation to leave the throng and bustle of the
street and spend a quiet half-hour in a worship-
ing assembly could not be resisted, and, entering, I found myself one of a large congregation
among whom were many men, young and old;
women of all ranks, from ladies richly and
fashionably attired to women whose clothing
marked them as toilers, some of them very poor.

It was a pleasant experience to join this sanctuary throng, and as I left the church, comforted and helped by the song, the prayers, the little sermon and the watchword chosen from the Bible, I felt glad that Christians are more and more inclining their hearts to keep with special attention the services of Lent.

I could not agree with an editorial which I read shortly after, in one of the daily papers, in which severe reflections were made on the declining piety of the Church of to-day. We live in a material age; an age of fierce business competition; a time when men struggle to amass money, when the contrasts between rich and poor are more sharply drawn than of old, when the besetting sin of the day is to bring matters to the test of human reason rather than to go in faith to the mercy seat and accept what God gives us there. But I remember the text of that day: "I am the Lord, the God of all flesh: is there anything too hard for me?" I see pressing in with insistent energy upon the Church a great and increasing throng of young men and women, student volunteers, who are ready and willing to give themselves to serve the Lord in any land where he may want them. I am aware that there is a large and increasing army of men and women who quietly read their Bibles and earnestly pray, and I do not believe that the Church is losing its hold upon the world, nor that Christ is deserting his own people.

After the forty days of Lent comes the dawn of the Easter morning. Once more with flowers and hymns of praise we enter our holy places; once more we hear sounding over every open grave, and hushing every rebellious thought in our hearts and soothing every grief, the words of him who still says to every one of us, "I am the Resurrection and the Life; he that believeth in me, though he were dead yet shall he live." Because our blessed Captain tasted death for every one of us, and himself took on his pale lips its utmost bitterness, the cup which the death angel holds to our lips is filled with the sweetness and flavor of everlasting life. This is the great joy of Easter. More and more, as we go on traveling the pilgrim road, we are conscious that it is but a road leading to another and an endless home. Along the road there are beautiful surprises. Friendship is ours, and domestic bliss; the dear love of kindred; the sweetness of companionship; the delight of standing shoulder to shoulder with comrades; the glory of service. But this is not our rest, and we are going on to that place where the beloved of the Lord shall dwell in safety by him and where they go no more out forever.

Somehow Easter always carries with it more of heaven than any other of the great anniversaries of the Christian year. In its first bright dawn the heavens were opened and the angels came down to comfort the weeping women and the disciples, mourning their Lord at the sepulcher, with those ecstatic words, "He is not here; he is risen!" It is more than a fancy, it is a precious fact, that the angels still come back to console the mourner, to strengthen the doubting, and to give Christ's own people the blessed assurance that he is with them still.

The festival of Easter comes to us at a propitious time, for, lo, the winter is past; the rain is over and gone; the time of the singing of birds is come; and the voice of the turtle is heard in our land. Winter, with its rigor and cold, its ice and frost and inclement blasts, its tempests on land and sea, is an emblem of warfare; its silence and sternness ally it to grief. Spring comes dancing and fluttering in with flowers and music and the blithe step of childhood. Her signs are evident before she is really here herself. First come the bluebirds, harbingers of a host; a little later there will be wrens and robins and orioles, and all the troop which make the woods musical and build sociably around our country homes.

Then the flowers will come. Happy are they who shall watch their whole procession, from the pussy-willow in March to the last blue gentian in October. We decorate our churches at Easter with the finest spoils of the hothouse—lilies, roses, palms, azaleas; nothing is too costly, nothing too lavish to be brought to the sanctuary or carried to the cemetery. Friend sends to friend the fragrant bouquet or the growing plant with the same tender significance which is evinced in the Christmas gifts, which carry from one heart to another a sweet message of love.

But God is giving us the Easter flowers in little hidden nooks in the forests, down by the corners of fences, in the sheltered places on the edges of the brook, and there we find the violet, the arbutus and other delicate blossoms which lead the van for the great army of nature's efflorescence. The first flowers are more delicately tinted and of shyer look and more ephemeral fragrance than those which come later. They are the Easter flowers. Later on we shall have millions of blossoms and more birds than we can count; now in the garden and the field we have enough to remind us that the winter is past, the rain is over and gone, the time of the singing of birds is come.

If any of us have been grieving over our own lack, over our sinful departure from God or over the loss of dear ones, let us at Easter forget the past, put our hand in that of our risen Lord, accept the sweetness of his voice and the gladness of his presence as he comes into our homes, and say, thankfully, as we hear his "Peace be unto you," "Lord, we are thine at this Easter time; we give ourselves to thee in a fullness which we have never known before. We are thine. Thine to use as thou wilt; thine to fill with blessing; thine to own. Take us, Lord, and so possess us with thyself that our waste places shall be glad, and the wilderness of our lives shall blossom as the rose." Such a prayer will find its way upward, and return to us in wonderful answers of blessing from the Lord.

Trustful To-morrows

After the chill of the winter—
  After the frost and rime—
The dance of the leaves,
The song in the eaves,
  And the waves like bells a-chime.

After the wide snow fleeces
  The green of the springing grass,
The buds uncreased
And the bees' sweet feast,
  And the ripple of winds that pass

CHAPTER XVII

MORNINGS WITH THE BIBLE

FOR most of us mornings with the Bible are rare. A few verses hastily read, or a chapter or two in the interval before breakfast, take up all the time we can give to the Word before the inflowing tide of the world is upon us. Yet few studies are so remunerative, few occupations are so delightful, and few duties are so imperative as daily attention to the Scriptures, and once convinced of the obligation, and in love with the engagement, most of us will so order our day that some part of it shall methodically be given to this employment.

"I want my Bible to be a living book," said a lady one day. "Yes, but it is already living," was her friend's response. "It is you who are not responsive."

Just as in organ and piano the music lies asleep, waiting the awakening touch of the performer's hand, so in chapter and text the sweet melodies lie, ready to start into choral and refrain when you come to them with loving and listening heart. To the color-blind the delicate shades of beauty in the spring or the autumnal landscape are not discernible; the lilacs and pinks and yellows and greens fail to show their wonderful variety of tint and hue. There are those who are dull of ear and dim of eye, they neither hear nor see, when the Bible is the book which is under their notice. It is to them merely an old volume to which they pay the tribute of a traditional reverence, or they regard it as an addition to the furnishing of the house, or else because their mothers loved it they sometimes lay upon it a caressing hand. But it is not *their* Bible, their daily food, their cup of cold water, their staff and stay, their very dearest dear of books.

We are bringing up, we in our Christian homes are bringing up, a generation of young people who have no intimate acquaintance with the Bible; who do not feel the obligation of its claim upon their thought and attention. Its precepts are not familiar to them by frequent repetition. Our hurried modern life, with its insistent clamor of trains and its schedules of business hours, has pushed the family altar out of many a home, so that children do not, as of old, twice a day read or listen to the reading of the Bible in household worship. The old Bible heroes, Moses, David, Samuel, Nehemiah, the Bible women, Ruth, Hannah, Deborah, Esther, are not any longer household words, and the sequence of the different books has dropped away from children's education. People remark glibly that they like the New Testament but do not care for the Old; which is very like saying that they like to live in the house but prefer to leave out the foundation. Of the treasures of history, of poetry, of learning, and of pure literature in our sacred Scriptures many persons are to-day pitifully and shamefully ignorant.

Now we may amend this by setting aside our daily hour—by preference a morning hour—for the reading of the Word. We shall love it only as we read it. We may do this by ourselves, or we may seek one or two congenial friends and together we may read and think upon what the Holy Spirit has set down for the instruction of the world through its every age.

A good plan is to take a single book and read it through at a sitting. Another good plan is to select a character and follow him through his career. If we choose to study the life of our Lord we may begin by looking at him first through the prophecies which foretold his coming, and then we may read the four stories of his earthly way as related by four men who lived with him and loved him. Then, following the closing chapters of St. John, we may read the history of the early church as given in the Book of Acts of the Apostles; then take up the letters sent by these good ministers to the congregations scattered abroad, so getting into our hearts true missionary fervor. Then, studying Hebrews, we may compare it with the Pentateuch, and musing and dreaming we may, with the blessed disciple whom Jesus loved, have a Revelation of the life to come.

Only, let us read and study the divine Word.

The "Literary Digest," some months ago, gave an interesting account of an experiment by which Dr. George A. Coe, professor of philosophy in Northwestern University, tested the Scriptural knowledge of certain college students. To a company of one hundred students he gave the following questions, requesting answers in writing:

1. What is the Pentateuch?

2. What is the higher criticism of the Scriptures?

3. Does the book of Jude belong to the New Testament, or to the Old?

4. Name one of the patriarchs of the Old Testament.

5. Name one of the judges of the Old Testament.

6. Name three of the kings of Israel.

7. Name three prophets.

8. Give one of the Beatitudes.

9. Quote a verse from the Letter to the Romans.

The answers received were all signed by the writers, and Professor Coe expresses his belief that they were, "without exception, sincere." In marking the answers as correct or incorrect Professor Coe put in the former class all that showed even a distant approach to definite knowledge, whether technical or only popular. He says (in an article in the "Christian Advocate") that ninety-six papers were returned, of which eight answered the nine questions correctly; thirteen papers answered eight questions correctly, eleven answered seven, five answered six, nine answered five, twelve answered four, eleven answered three, thirteen answered two, eleven answered one, and three answered none. The number giving a correct answer to the first question was sixty, to the second, sixteen; to the third, fifty-six; to the fourth, sixty-one; to the fifth, forty-five; to the sixth, forty-seven; to the seventh, fifty-two; to the eighth, seventy-six; to the ninth, thirty-one.

Ninety-six papers, with nine answers on each, give us a total of eight hundred and sixty-four answers. The total number of correct answers was four hundred and forty-four, a little over one-half.

Nearly two-thirds of them knew what the Pentateuch is, but only one-sixth of them knew what the "higher criticism" is; and only one-third could quote a single verse from the Epistle to the Romans.

Would it not be well for us, in test of ourselves as well as to induce our young friends, to submit in a similar way to some such trial of our accurate knowledge of the Bible?

CHAPTER XVIII

SWEET HOUR OF PRAYER

"O LORD of life and Lord of love, love us into life and give us life to love thee. Grant us life enough to put life into all things; that when we travel o'er this part of our life, and it seems but dust and barrenness, we may be of those who hope in thee. Touch this barrenness till all things bloom. Touch those of us whose life is barrener than it need be, lacking knowledge and beauty, filled with petty interests and foolish cares. Lord, forgive us that our life is so poor, and grant us the thoughts of God, that we may be enabled for the time to come to make this very desert blossom as the rose. Grant that in us, short-lived, vexed with cares, hungry, thirsty, dying, the spirit of God may so come that the beauty of the Lord our God may be upon us, and the work of our hands be established through Jesus Christ our Lord."

This prayer of George Dawson breathes the desire of every soul that, out of want and weakness and penury, turns to the Lord for help and strength and affluent bounty. How should burdens be borne, how should sins be pardoned, how should wisdom be found, if there were no still hour when we might seek the Lord?

In our extremity is always God's opportunity. Strangely do we limit our Lord's goodness and power when we hesitate to carry everything to him in prayer; our spiritual needs not only, but our temporal requirements. Our food and raiment, the roof over our heads, the shoes for the children's feet, the health we find failing in our loved ones or ourselves, the journey we wish to take, the choice of a school or a college for son or daughter, the business decision we must make, these are legitimate objects of prayer. Our Father knoweth of what we have need before we ask him, yet he says, "Ask, and it shall be given; seek, and ye shall find;" and desires that we inquire of him concerning his will.

All prayer, to be real, must be genuine; sincere; the utterance of the heart. It must be believing prayer. It must be penitent prayer. Also it must be made in the dear name of Christ, and in submission to the will of God. "Not my will, but thine," cries the devout soul.

Father John, that fine old mystic of the

Greek church, says, "Only feel truly and sincerely your need of that for which you pray, and believe that it comes from God, and you will obtain anything and everything. For with God all things are possible. Whether you are sitting down, or walking abroad, or thinking, or writing, or working; whether you are well or ill, at home or out, on land or on sea, be continually assured that God at that moment is wholly with you; that he hears the finest breathings and beatings of your hearts; and that he listens to hear and help you. Has he not said to you that he waits to be gracious to you? Forget, deny, despair of anything and everything but that. Remember that for Omnipotence nothing is difficult, nor for Love a trouble or a task. All things, therefore, whatsoever you shall ask in prayer, believing, you shall surely receive."

Prayer is not always selfish asking. Some, and a large part of it, is intercession for others; and whoso intercedes for the soul of his friend follows closely the example and obeys the command of the Master. Some of it is adoration. Some of it is praise. Some of it is just a simple, silent, sweet drawing nigh unto God. Of one thing may we be assured: that only as we do often, and closely, and earnestly, give ourselves into God's care, committing our way unto him, asking his direction, floating out upon the infinite sea of his grace, shall we grow in the Christian life. To pray is to think of Jesus; to think of Jesus is to become acquainted with God.

There is a little picture poem by Francis Fisher Browne which often returns to me when I remember those who have parted with their childhood's simple faith, those who no longer kneel down at morning or at night to say their prayers:

> Upon the white sea sand
> There sat a pilgrim band
> Telling the losses that their lives had known,
> While evening waned away
> From breezy cliff and bay,
> And the strong tide went out with weary moan.
>
> One spake, with quivering lip,
> Of a fair freighted ship
> With all his household to the deep gone down;
> But one had wilder woe
> For a fair face long ago
> Lost in the darker depths of a great town.
>
> There were who mourned their youth
> With a most loving ruth
> For its brave hopes and memories ever green;
> And one upon the West
> Turned an eye that would not rest
> For far-off hills whereon its joy had been.

Some talked of vanished gold,
Some of proud honors told,
Some spake of friends that were their trust no more;
And one of a green grave
Beside a foreign wave,
That made him sit so lonely on the shore.

But when their tales were done
There spake among them one,
A stranger, seeming from all sorrow free—
"Sad losses have ye met
But mine is heavier yet,
For a believing heart hath gone from me."

"Alas!" these pilgrims said,
"For the living and the dead,
For fortune's cruelty, for love's sure cross,
For the wrecks of land and sea!
But, however it came to thee,
Thine, stranger, is life's last and heaviest loss."

Whatever else the world may give it can give us no better thing than the hour of prayer. Whatever it may take, it cannot rob us of peace if that dear hour is still our refuge.

CHAPTER XIX

Growing Old

Perhaps the keenest pang a woman ever feels is in the day she realizes that her youth has gone. She seldom reaches this knowledge without some external sign or token. It is in the frankness of a friend who, meeting her, after the lapse of years, observes her altered looks, and comments on them, "You have changed. I would never have known you!" It is in the over-officious courtesy of the fellow passenger on a railway train or cable car, who, yielding her a seat, kindly explains that he cannot suffer an old lady to stand. It is in the reflection of her mirror, which shows her gray hair and a hollowing cheek, or in the merciless fidelity of the camera, which reveals differences she had not remarked. Yet, once confessed, once admitted on friendly terms, age has its advantages. The elderly woman may go unchallenged wherever she will. She may form her friendships on an equal plane with people older and younger than herself. Boys and girls come to

her for counsel. The love affairs of the family
are related to her, and as under her silver hair
she has a warm heart, often absurdly young
though nobody suspects it, she is a wise and
a safe confidante.

Often for many years the middle aged and
elderly woman enjoys firm health and is the
possessor of vigor to which her youth was a
stranger. She shrinks from no undertaking,
she is afraid of no task; she goes gaily across
the continent or around the globe. You find
her peering into Dakota dug-outs and Indian
tepees; she is admitted into Hindu zenanas and
Japanese homes. She understands life, and
reads other women by her own wide experience.

If she is married, and her husband, growing
old with her, has kept pace with her in mind
and thought—though it sometimes happens
that a woman, having more leisure, outgrows
her hard-working husband—then the two in the
serenity of their life's evening are as happy as
two children. They have lived and loved together. They may sit often and long in silence,
having no need of speech: there is an inti-
macy which depends not on language for
interpretation.

Growing old is less a terror than it used to be, for less than formerly are old people laid upon the shelf. The well-meant but mistaken kindness of their juniors is apt to deprive aged members of a household of the work they like to do, and they gradually feel that they are first unimportant and next encumbrances. No greater blunder is ever made than that which thus grieves persons who, after lives of much activity, feel themselves crowded out and pushed aside by the newer generation.

Augustus Hare has an inimitable sketch of a clever old lady, one Mrs. Duncan Stewart, who until long past eighty held a sort of social court. Of her pains and aches this sturdy gentlewoman refused to speak. "Take care," she would say to a contemporary who had a tendency thus to complain, "or you will become that most dreadful of all things, a self-observant valetudinarian." It would be well for everyone to make this admirable rule his or her own. We gain nothing by discussing our maladies, and we often bring upon ourselves the very physical pangs we dread by fixing them on our mental retina.

Of two things those who are growing old

should be extremely careful. One is to neglect
no little point of decorum. Manners are as
beautiful in age as in youth, and no burden of
years can really excuse brusqueness, or harsh-
ness, or inattention to courtesy. A lady told
me of a visit she paid to a great-uncle one hundred and one years of age. When she was taking her leave her aged relative said, "My dear
niece, I beg that you will pardon me, in that the
infirmities of my age prevent my accompanying
you to the door." Was not that beautiful? To
a gentleman of ninety a young woman carried
an offering of lovely flowers. "How kind and
sweet," he said, "is this thoughtfulness of yours.
You, so young, bring roses to me, so old!"

Then, let the old lady and the old gentleman
dress as neatly and with as much elegance as
possible. Careful dress, clothing as rich as the
purse can afford, is more necessary to age than
to youth. When I was a girl I had a bonnet
trimmed with pink roses. Said a dear old gentlewoman, "You do not need those trimmings,
dear; the roses are in your cheeks. Wait till
you are older, to put on the gayer dress."

The old should associate with the young, and
should have tolerance for the views of the latter

while trenchantly holding fast to their own prerogatives. I know an octogenarian who still practices successfully his learned profession, keeping abreast with younger men and going to Europe, summer after summer, alone, for purposes of recreation and study. Another, not so far from ninety, comes from a country home three times a week to read in a great library, traveling eighty miles a day for the purpose. These men have known how to grow old gracefully. They are of those who prove to us, with Browning, that "the best is yet to be."

Old people are precious links with yesterday. When I talk with one whose memory goes back to days when New York society found its center on the Battery, and Chicago was a mere wilderness with Indians pitching wigwams beside its lake, the past grows very vivid.

On the path the old are treading we shall soon follow them. Of one thing we may be sure, Time is the great conqueror, and imperceptibly his gentle hand is snatching away the youth from us all.

CHAPTER XX

Home Awaiting

It is the dearest word in our language, that sweet word Home. Born of our deepest need, answering to a responsive chord in our nature, whatever the accident of our environment or the peculiarity of our training there is a homing instinct which sends us back from the farthest wandering on the face of the earth to the old fireside and the mother's chair. When annually we of this land keep our Thanksgiving feast, every train across the continent, every ship that sails the sea, bears freight of loving hearts, carries home again the men and women who, from business, study and pleasure, turn yearningly and wistfully to the place where they played in childhood.

All through our changeful days we are bound by strong and slender though often invisible threads to the home of our bringing up, to the earliest associations. Yet death is all the while slowly or swiftly obliterating earthly scenes, and men come and go, and families pass away, and

it is ever true, here in this world, of everything
we see and hear, that the wind passeth over it
and it is gone, and that the place which knows
us to-day may soon know us no more. Realizing
this more and more as our experiences multiply
and a deeper note comes into our lives, we look
forward to the home which shall abide, to the
immortal land "conjubilant with song."

> "Jerusalem the golden,
>   With milk and honey blest,
> Beneath thy contemplation
>   Sink heart and voice opprest.
> I know not, O, I know not,
>   What social joys are there,
> What radiancy of glory,
>   What bliss beyond compare.
>
> "There is the throne of David,
>   And there, from care released,
> The song of them that triumph,
>   The shout of them that feast."

Our dear Lord, leaving his disciples lonely
and bewildered, not knowing what they should
do without his presence and the comfort of his
gentle strength, said, "In my Father's house are
many mansions. I go to prepare a place for
you." There and then he named the home
awaiting us after the trials and storms of this
world; it is the Father's house, and where else

should the children gather and where else
should there be provision so abundant for their
every want!

In the Father's house all the lost children
shall find one another; all the brothers and sisters will sit down together in the gladness of reunion after separation. Never let anyone for
an instant imagine that our home is to be a mere
state of blessedness, a sort of Nirvana, a beatific
sphere of isolation; it is to be the rallying place
of the kindred, the joyous hearth round which
we shall meet when task and toil are over, and
unfettered, without handicap or limitation, we
shall go on, learning, loving, living, forever.

Here, a thousand obstacles interfere with us
and a thousand hindrances interpose to prevent
our development. We have feet, not wings.
Inherited tendencies clog our noblest efforts,
our aspirations are weighted by the grossness of
appetite, our good is marred by evil. Sin
creeps into our most beautiful Edens. Home
life is shadowed by frowning faces, by uncongenial dispositions, by tempers which flare up
into sudden flame, or smoke and smolder in
gloomy wrath.

One is never sure, when a day begins, what

may lie in its pathway before nightfall. One is never able to say precisely how he shall meet temptation, nor to count on his reinforcements. Needs must we sometimes strive with Apollyon and find him bearing us down with bitter onset and terrific blows. There, the core of all the sweetness will be entire freedom from sin, entire absence of the evil overmastering desire, entire conformity to the divine will, and joy in obeying the divine commands.

It is certain that in the home awaiting us we shall have service of the highest. In what way we shall serve, on what errands be sent, we do not know, but we shall know hereafter. With the glad alacrity of children we shall carry messages and study new lessons and do as the Father bids us, once we are safe within the gates of the Father's house.

Sometimes we wonder, foolishly, whether we shall know our loved ones when we meet them again. As if the life likeness would be gone simply because the dear ones had been dwelling a little longer than ourselves in the Father's presence! As if love were a thing of the hour! As if death were more than transition, the angel of emancipation, the opener of the door into the lighted room after the long journey! As if it were God's way to give us a half blessing! The joy of the home awaiting us will be the joy of meeting once more and keeping through eternity the little ones who went on before us, the comrades and friends who dropped away from our side, the fathers and mothers who showed us first the pathway to our God. Faith claims this dear privilege of anticipation. There, in the Father's house, we shall meet, we shall love, we shall serve, we shall know and be known.

> "For death is but a covered way
> That opens into light,
> Wherein no blinded child can stray
> Beyond the Father's sight."

Best of all, in the home awaiting us we shall see our Master face to face. How wonderful will be that glad recognition. Not as they saw him who walked with him in Galilee, when he bore the burden of our flesh and was acquainted with grief; not as the disciples and the women who came to him for healing and help saw him, with glory veiled and hidden; but rather as those privileged ones beheld him to whom he came after his resurrection, entering into their company and saying "Peace!" when the doors were shut, and their wistful eyes could scarce believe in the divine beauty of that strange revelation. We shall see Jesus enthroned and glorified. We shall hear his voice. There will be no dimming cloud of sin to keep us away, but even as he draws us to him we shall hasten, happy to be in that close circle of those who are evermore his own.

Says Jeremy Taylor:

"If thou wilt be fearless of death endeavor to be in love with the felicities of saints and angels and be once persuaded to believe that there is a condition of living better than this; that there are creatures more noble than we; that above there is a country better than ours; that the inhabitants know more and know better, and are in places of rest and desire; and first learn to value it, and then learn to purchase it, and death cannot be a formidable thing which lets us into so much joy and so much felicity.

"And indeed who would not think his own condition mended if he passed from conversing with dull mortals, with ignorant and foolish persons, with tyrants, and enemies of learning, to converse with Homer and Plato, with Socrates and Cicero, with Plutarch and Fabricius? So the heathens speculated, but we consider higher. 'The dead that die in the Lord' shall converse with St. Paul, and all the college of the Apostles, and all the saints and martyrs, with all the good men whose memory we preserve in honor, with excellent kings and holy bishops, and with the great Shepherd and Bishop of our souls, Jesus Christ, and with God himself. For 'Christ died for us, that, whether we wake or sleep, we might live together with him.' Then we shall be free from lust and envy, from fear and rage, from covetousness and sorrow, from tears and cowardice: and these indeed properly are the only evils that are contrary to felicity and wisdom."

I think we limit our conception of heaven too strictly to the devotional side of our nature, as if we were to spend eternity simply and exclusively in acts of worship. That praise will be the atmosphere of our being, that our souls will be bathed in thankfulness, who can doubt? But, if we are to go onward in the future as in the present life, we shall share social converse and peer into the secret things of God. Science, in its infancy here, will be studied there in beautiful unfoldings, with powers freed from the cobwebs of earth. We shall go on learning with open eye and quickened ear. Think of learning without fatigue, of dwelling where all around assists the mind, of going at an instant's notice to the farthest star! There is no reason to fear that we shall be hindered in heaven from pursuing any employment which may be carried on in the pure sight of God.

We are flitting, as the call reaches us, from these houses of clay to our everlasting habitations.

"Not rising up together
  In whirlwind or in cloud,
In the hush of the summer weather
  Or when storms are gathering loud,
But one by one we go
To the sweetness none may know."

A messenger straight from the City of God crosses our threshold, and one dear to us is not, for God has taken him. The messenger comes to us one by one, and we know not when; but let it be at cockcrow, or at noon, or at midnight, it is the summons home, and the Lord himself will lead us to the place prepared. An end then of every anxiety, a realization then of all for which we have hoped and waited and prayed. We shall be with God in heaven forever.

"We are on our journey home
  Where Christ our Lord has gone,
We shall meet around his throne
  When he makes his people one
In the new Jerusalem.

"O glory shining far
  From the never setting sun,
O trembling Morning Star,
  Our journey's almost done
To the new Jerusalem."
                    180

CHAPTER XXI

A STUDY OF ANGELS

THE Bible is a supernatural book, and its pages are bright with supernatural radiance. All through its course, from Genesis to Revelation, we hear the rustling of angel wings, and behold the shimmering of angel robes, and hear the sweet cadences of seraph voices. In these duller days we are often insensible to the vision and the song, and we do not readily accept the sweet comfort the Lord is ever willing to send us, but why should we refuse to believe the old never repealed word which says that he giveth his angels charge concerning us, that in their hands they bear us up, and that they so guard us that we do not hurt our feet upon the way, nor stumble, nor fall? Are they not all ministering spirits, still sent forth to minister to them who shall be heirs of salvation?

The first recorded mention of an angelic errand to our race was not, however, one of comfort or help, but of restraint, and of the barred

13   181

door of a lost Eden. "And the Lord God said, Behold, the man is become as one of us, to know good and evil; and now, lest he put forth his hand, and take also of the tree of life, and eat, and live forever: therefore the Lord God sent him forth from the garden of Eden, to till the ground from whence he was taken. So he drove out the man; and he placed at the east of the garden of Eden the Cherubim, and the flame of a sword which turned every way, to keep the way of the tree of life."

Terrible in their glory, these mighty creatures of Jehovah, created perhaps for the purpose which they then fulfilled, stood still at Eden's morning gate, with the glory of the dawn light on their faces. And man, fleeing from their blinding radiance and dumb before the majesty of that circling sword of fire, might still look up to heaven, from angel and from brand, and discern, faint indeed, and dim in the distance, but strange and clear and steadfast, the promise of the coming Saviour, whose star should yet shine in the East.

When Moses, listening to the voice of the Lord, told the children of Israel to make unto the Lord an offering of their best and choicest possessions and to prepare for him a tabernacle and a sanctuary, we again find the cherubim, symbolizing now the covenant love of God to man. This time the cherubim are to be made of fine beaten gold, and the Lord himself gives the pattern to Moses. "Of one piece with the mercy-seat shall ye make the cherubim on the two ends thereof. And the cherubim shall spread out their wings on high, covering the mercy-seat with their wings, with their faces one to another; toward the mercy-seat shall the faces of the cherubim be." Through the long ages before Immanuel came, priest and prophet and the devout and expectant among God's people, praying for the Messiah, knew that the glory of the overshadowing cherubim was as the glory of the New Jerusalem in the Holy of Holies. There it abode until that dark day on Golgotha when by wicked hands the Messiah, whom his own did not recognize, was crucified and slain, and then, when the veil of the temple was rent, and the saints lying in their graves arose and appeared unto many, for ever and for ever the glory faded from the place where the cherubim had kept their century upon century's tryst.

It was while sitting under the oaks of Mamre,

in his tent door, in the heat of the day, that
Abraham the aged suddenly had a vision of
angels. Perhaps he had been musing of the
wonderful way over which the Lord had led him
from the days of his youth, when the mystic call
had drawn him away from his kindred and his
father's house to seek an unknown land. The
Lord had promised Abraham many things; as
yet the fulfillment of a part of the promise was
delayed. His beautiful wife, Sarah, no longer
hoped to be the mother of his son; she had fore-
gone that proud desire, and, jealous as she was
of Hagar, the disdainful Egyptian, she had
acknowledged Hagar's child as the heir of her
husband's line. The transaction with Hagar,
read by modern Occidental eyes, is incompre-
hensible, but it was and is in keeping with ordinary Oriental usage, and no doubt even Sarah
took a certain pleasure in the beauty and vigor
of the Egyptian's boy.

God had distinctly told Abraham that Sarah
his wife, a fair woman still, but ninety years
old, should bear him a son. And Abraham be-
lieved God. Yet it may well have been that
under his faith there was the moaning cry at
times of impatience with the long waiting; and

again, that there may have been the human pro-
test at what seemed an impossibility; as though
anything could ever be impossible to God! As
Abraham sat there, quietly thinking, he lifted
up his eyes, and lo! three men stood over against
him. They had not approached. The long
white stretch of sand had no footprints upon
it, and no caravan had brought these messengers, on whose garments there was no dust of
travel, in whose benignant faces was no shadow
of fatigue. There were three men, but one was
evidently the chief and the others his attendants; and it may well have been that this kingly
one was our Lord Christ, appearing thus as
again and again he appeared to his servants
before he took upon him our flesh and lived
among us for three and thirty years.

"My lord," said the patriarch, bowing low
with Oriental courtesy, "if now I have found
favor in thy sight, pass not away, I pray thee,
from thy servant: let now a little water be
fetched, and wash your feet, and rest yourselves
under the tree: and I will fetch a morsel of
bread, and comfort ye your heart; after that ye
shall pass on: forasmuch as ye are come to your
servant." Then followed the remarkable inter-

view in which Isaac was again promised, and the still more amazing conversation in which Abraham pleaded for Sodom, over which impended the wrath of Jehovah. In all history there is nothing more extraordinary than the story of Abraham's long and intimate talk with the Lord, its pleading tenderness and compassion on the part of the man and its gracious relenting on the part of God. Intercessory prayer has here its pattern and its encouragement.

The Lord, if indeed one angel was the Lord, returned to heaven, and only the two serving angels went to Sodom and met Lot sitting in the gate of that wicked and doomed city. For consolation and for joy the theophany might be given, for warning and for destruction it was enough to send forth the angels of war and of death.

Years afterward, when Isaac was a fair boy, a lad on whom his father's passionate love was set, that father felt that the divine command required him to offer up Isaac as a sacrifice. But just as the knife was raised to slay the child God interfered, and from the rifted skies the 'Angel of the Lord spoke and stayed the father's hand. And to Hagar in the desert, fainting, wearied, utterly dismayed and heart-stricken, an angel came saying, "What aileth thee, Hagar?" And God opened her tear-blinded eyes, and she saw the water of salvation, the well with its fragrant waves, and she filled her bottle with water, and gave the lad drink.

More beautiful than almost any other story in the Book is that of the sleeping Jacob on his way to Padan-aram, home and mother and father behind him, with all that home meant to the quiet peace-loving nature; an estranged twin-brother, deceived and wronged, also behind him; but in his heart, with all its sinfulness, a true appreciation of and a real longing for the Divine. How lovely is the narrative so simply and quaintly told in the words of Scripture:

"And Jacob went out from Beer-sheba, and went toward Haran. And he lighted upon a certain place, and tarried there all night, because the sun was set; and he took of the stones of that place, and put them for his pillows, and lay down in that place to sleep. And he dreamed, and behold a ladder set up on the earth, and the top of it reached to heaven: and behold the angels of God ascending and descending on it. And, behold, the Lord stood above it, and said,

I am the Lord God of Abraham thy father, and the God of Isaac: the land whereon thou liest, to thee will I give it, and to thy seed; and thy seed shall be as the dust of the earth; and thou shalt spread abroad to the west, and to the east, and to the north, and to the south: and in thee and in thy seed shall all the families of the earth be blessed. And, behold, I am with thee, and will keep thee in all places whither thou goest, and will bring thee again into this land; for I will not leave thee, until I have done that which I have spoken to thee of. And Jacob awaked out of his sleep, and he said, Surely the Lord is in this place; and I knew it not. And he was afraid, and said, How dreadful is this place! this is none other but the house of God, and this is the gate of heaven. And Jacob rose up early in the morning, and took the stone that he had put for his pillows, and set it up for a pillar, and poured oil upon the top of it. And he called the name of that place Beth-el: but the name of that city was called Luz at the first. And Jacob vowed a vow, saying, If God will be with me, and will keep me in this way that I go, and will give me bread to eat, and raiment to put on, so that I come again to my father's house in peace;

then shall the Lord be my God: and this stone, which I have set for a pillar, shall be God's house: and of all that thou shalt give me I will surely give the tenth unto thee."

Observe how the ladder, invisible to us, reaches from earth to heaven. Is it not thus reaching still? And to and fro the angels go, upon its shining rounds, doing the will of God. With what grace of thankfulness the young man pledges his gift of acknowledgment, that tribute of the tenth—which is surely little enough for any of us to give to the Lord whose watchful care of us, too, never ceases.

Faber's familiar hymn, sung in our churches and at family worship, never loses its charm:

"Hark! Hark! my soul, angelic songs are swelling
  O'er earth's green fields and ocean's wave-beat shore:
How sweet the truth those blessed strains are telling
  Of that new life when sin shall be no more!
      Angels of Jesus, angels of light,
      Singing to welcome the pilgrims of the night.

"Darker than night life's shadows fall around us,
  And like benighted men we miss our mark;
God hides himself, and grace hath scarcely found us
  Ere death finds out his victims in the dark.

"Onward we go, for still we hear them singing,
  'Come, weary souls, for Jesus bids you come!'
And through the dark, its echoes sweetly ringing,
  The music of the gospel leads us home.

"Far, far away, like bells at evening pealing,
  The voice of Jesus sounds o'er land and sea,
And laden souls by thousands, meekly stealing,
  Kind Shepherd! turn their weary steps to thee.

"Rest comes at length, though life be long and dreary;
  The day must dawn and darksome night be past;
All journeys end in welcome to the weary,
  And heaven, the heart's true home, will come at last.

"Cheer up, my soul! faith's moonbeams softly glisten
  Upon the breast of life's most troubled sea;
And it will cheer thy drooping heart to listen
  To those brave songs which angels mean for thee.

"Angels, sing on! your faithful watches keeping;
  Sing us sweet fragments of the songs above;
While we toil on, and soothe ourselves with weeping,
  Till life's long night shall break in endless love.
      Angels of Jesus, angels of light,
      Singing to welcome the pilgrims of the night!"

Many long days and nights pass over Jacob's
head; he toils and waits and loves in the house
of his stern kinsman Laban, the Syrian.   The
sweetest idyl of love and patience in the world
is that old story of Jacob's passion for Rachel.
"And Jacob served seven years for Rachel, and
they seemed to him but a few days for the love
he had to her."   Yet seven more were appointed
unto him, fourteen in all, before the dearly beloved became his bride.

We do not know how often the angels
strengthened Jacob during those years of exile

and persistent labor, but they came, if inference
may count, many a time and oft; sometimes in
companies, sometimes singly. Once, indeed, to
this child of God there was given an experience
of depth and agony in prayer such as few of our
race have ever known.

"And Jacob was left alone; and there wrestled
a man with him until the breaking of the day.
And when he saw that he prevailed not against
him, he touched the hollow of his thigh; and the
hollow of Jacob's thigh was strained, as he
wrestled with him. And he said, Let me go, for
the day breaketh. And he said, I will not let
thee go, except thou bless me. And he said unto
him, What is thy name? And he said, Jacob.
And he said, Thy name shall be called no more
Jacob, but Israel: for thou hast striven with
God and with men, and hast prevailed. And
Jacob asked him, and said, Tell me, I pray thee,
thy name. And he said, Wherefore is it that
thou dost ask after my name? And he blessed
him there. And Jacob called the name of the
place Peniel: for, said he, I have seen God face
to face, and my life is preserved. And the sun
rose upon him as he passed over Penuel, and he
halted upon his thigh. Therefore the children

of Israel eat not the sinew of the hip which is upon the hollow of the thigh, unto this day: because he touched the hollow of Jacob's thigh in the sinew of the hip."

We remember the circumstances which confronted Jacob: the menace of his offended brother on the advance to meet him with his band of followers, armed to the teeth, ready to pounce upon and destroy the caravan and to avenge the injury of the long ago, when Jacob by deceit carried off the blessing and the birthright. Says the Rev. Dr. Wm. M. Baker, writing of this night of agonizing prayer:

"How very much more do we know of this Visitor than did Jacob! Whatever those learned who had him as companion during the seven theophanies which came after this is ours also. All that men came to know of Christ during his life and death, ages after, on earth, is our own. Imagine our importunity to have increased up to the measure of our information! Though our Esau is Satan, and with all hell at his heels, what need we fear, having such an interlocked grasp upon our Lord!

"We read of how a king or emperor knights upon some well-fought field some valiant soldier, the nobility of whose new title is borne by his rejoicing children to the end of time. So is it here; the distinctive name of the people of God, till at last prayer shall perish, is 'the Israel of God.' 'An Israelite indeed,' said Jesus of Nathanael, since beneath the fig-tree he had himself been wrestled with by the man in prayer: Nathanael, like Jacob, being permitted so soon afterward to see the face of this divine Foe—Jesus, the Christ.

"And Jacob is blessed of the Son of God. But, now as ever, not one syllable does Christ say as to how, and when, and where, the suppliant—in this case Jacob—shall be rescued from his Esau. The patriarch knows, as he advances next day alone and at the forefront of his household, nothing but that God is with him; and to him he leaves it all. None the less he still uses all possible means, bowing himself seven times before the savage sheik who, with his four hundred spears at his back, bears down upon him. Here is no interposition of God! Esau rides down upon his traitorous brother with leveled spear; his vengeance whetted by the sight of his enemy, his lust for plunder by the swarming herds and slaves in full view.

There is no faltering in a purpose which during near half a hundred years has hardened into steel. With eye and weapon unswerving Esau rushes down upon Jacob. A moment more and the unarmed man will lie weltering in his blood —his wives and sons, his flocks and herds, given over to slaughter, outrage, and spoil.

"In that instant Esau is struck through the heart! But it is by an arrow peculiar to the quiver and bow of him of whom it is written: 'Thine arrows are sharp in the hearts of the king's enemies, whereby the people are subdued under thee!' For it is an arrow of conquering love! Saul, the persecutor, fell transfixed by it when in full career, and so is it now. 'And Esau ran to meet him, and embraced him, and fell on his neck and kissed him; and they wept.'"

Friends, there come to us, in our lives, periods as pregnant with calamity as this period which came to Jacob. Again and again we are perplexed, harassed, troubled, distressed, but ah! never, never, forsaken if we believe in God, if we dare to take him at his word, if we carry every trial and trouble and disaster and threat of evil straight to his feet. When we are tempted he can enable us to conquer, when we are overcome he can help us to arise. Again let us quote from Dr. Baker, whose thought of the personal Christ was so vivid and his realization of Christ's immanence so precious that, with the saints of old, he seems to have had the open vision:

"'The kingdom of heaven suffereth violence, and the violent take it by force.' Jacob saw a ladder, reaching from where he lay to heaven, up and down which trooped the angels: he is afterward to learn that this is as a scaling ladder planted upon the soil, its top against the ramparts of heaven, and by which he and we must storm heaven itself or do without. If you who read have never known of the almost infinite stringency of the world upon you, and at every step; if you have not gone to God and prayed and prayed, and prayed only apparently to be repulsed—yes, and seemingly cruelly repulsed, and often—you have no business with this page. It is to such as have known, long known, the agony of prayer long despised, rejected, refused, these lines are addressed. For it is not 'the kingdom,' it is the King of heaven who 'suffereth violence,' who must be taken by force. Our want is but the temporary inducement to that

which is the supreme thing: and that is, our so
wrestling in prevailing prayer with the Son of
God as to expand and develop our whole
nature into likeness to his. Thus are we 'made
partakers of the divine nature;' thus are we, in
the end, 'filled with all the fullness of God.' "

In the New Testament we find the angels in
constant ministry upon our Lord. An angel
announced to the Virgin the honor of her coming motherhood: "Fear not, Mary: for thou hast
found favor with God." A choir of angels sang
in the hearing of the shepherds on the night of
Immanuel's birth:

"And there were shepherds in the same country abiding in the field, and keeping watch by
night over their flock. And an angel of the
Lord stood by them, and the glory of the Lord
shone round about them: and they were sore
afraid. And the angel said unto them, Be not
afraid; for behold, I bring you good tidings of
great joy which shall be to all the people: for
there is born to you this day in the city of David
a Saviour, which is Christ the Lord. And this
is the sign unto you; Ye shall find a babe
wrapped in swaddling clothes, and lying in a
manger. And suddenly there was with the angel

The Annunciation.   (After the Painting by D. G. Rossetti.)

a multitude of the heavenly host praising God, and saying,

"Glory to God in the highest,
"And on earth peace among men in whom he
is well pleased.

"And it came to pass, when the angels went away from them into heaven, the shepherds said one to another, Let us now go even unto Bethlehem, and see this thing that is come to pass, which the Lord hath made known unto us. And they came with haste, and found both Mary and Joseph, and the babe lying in the manger. And when they saw it, they made known concerning the saying which was spoken to them about this child. And all that heard it wondered at the things which were spoken unto them by the shepherds. But Mary kept all these sayings, pondering them in her heart. And the shepherds returned, glorifying and praising God for all the things that they had heard and seen, even as it was spoken unto them.

"And when eight days were fulfilled for circumcising him, his name was called Jesus, which was so called by the angel before he was conceived in the womb."

Our Lord had the angels ever within his call;

they were doubtless awed and amazed when they beheld his humiliation, but their business, as was his, supremely, was to do God's will fully, and without a question. And so when he needed them they ministered to him: in the lonely nights upon the cold still mountains, in the desert spaces, in the garden of his agony. Angels said, as they waited to see his disciples in the dawn of the resurrection, "He is not here. He is risen!" and when he ascended, and a cloud received him out of the sight of his friends and followers, while yet they stood steadfastly gazing into heaven as he went, behold two men stood by them in white apparel, saying, "This Jesus shall so come in like manner as ye beheld him going into heaven."

Very dear to every Christian heart must be that story of Peter shut up in prison by Herod while prayer was made earnestly by the church unto God for him.

"And when Herod was about to bring him forth, the same night Peter was sleeping between two soldiers, bound with two chains: and guards before the door kept the prison. And behold, an angel of the Lord stood by him, and a light shined in the cell: and he smote Peter on

the side, and awoke him, saying, Rise up quickly.
And his chains fell off from his hands. And the
angel said unto him, Gird thyself, and bind
on thy sandals.''

As if the angel had said gently to the prisoner,
"Take thy time; there is no need of haste.
Herod shall not bring thee forth for death.
Jehovah Jesus gives thee life to serve him yet
a while longer here."

"And he saith unto him, Cast thy garment
about thee, and follow me. And he went out,
and followed; and he wist not that it was true
which was done by the angel, but thought he saw
a vision. And when they were past the first and
the second ward, they came unto the iron gate
that leadeth into the city; which opened to them
of its own accord: and they went out, and passed
on through one street; and straightway the angel departed from him. And when Peter was
come to himself, he said, Now I know of a truth,
that the Lord hath sent forth his angel and de-
livered me out of the hand of Herod, and from
all the expectation of the people of the Jews.
And when he had considered the thing, he came
to the house of Mary the mother of John whose
surname was Mark; where many were gathered

together and were praying. And when he
knocked at the door of the gate, a maid came to
answer, named Rhoda. And when she knew
Peter's voice, she opened not the gate for joy,
but ran in, and told that Peter stood before the
gate. And they said unto her, Thou art mad.
But she confidently affirmed that it was even so.
And they said, It is his angel. But Peter continued knocking: and when they had opened,
they saw him, and were amazed. But he, beckoning unto them with the hand to hold their
peace, declared unto them how the Lord had
brought him forth out of the prison. And he
said, Tell these things unto James, and to the
brethren. And he departed, and went to another
place."

Not to you and me in these later times is it
appointed often that the angels shall bring their
hands of potency and break open our prison
doors in our sight; yet I am not doubtful that
they do come, and that when our doors of trouble
open of their own accord it is because God's
angels have been here to oil their hinges and
noiselessly turn their locks. To many a dear one
in the last hour of earthly life our Lord sends
his angels, and they come in compassion and

give the needed aid. And to an angel whatever God bids is important; his errand to a hovel is as welcome as his message to a palace. The Eastern legend of the angel sent from God to give counsel to King Solomon and also to help on her way back to her people a little yellow ant, burdened with a heavy load, has its lesson for us.

But once we are freed from the body and its limitations, once we are safe at home, not an angel, however strong and beautiful—not Gabriel, nor Ithuriel, nor Michael—shall lead us into the great peace; but the Lamb that was slain, our blessed Redeemer, shall himself conduct us to the green pastures and the still waters.

To Moses, to Gideon, to Elijah, to Daniel, to Peter, to John, even to the incarnate Jesus himself, the angels came at need. To the saints, ransomed by the precious blood and brought home to go no more out, the Lord of the angels shall give the sweet welcome, where

> "Ten thousand times ten thousand,
>   In sparkling raiment bright,
> The armies of the ransomed saints
>   Throng up the steeps of light.
> 'Tis finished, all is finished,
>   Their fight with death and sin.
> Fling open wide the golden gates,
>   And let the victors in!"

CHAPTER XXII

Talking With Our Heavenly Father

Prayer is too often narrowed into a mere begging of favors from God. We are in want of many things; of health, of a business opening, of ease of mind, of judgment so that we may make right decisions. We are solicitous for our loved ones; we do not know what is best for them and we are afraid of making mistakes, or they are ill and we long for their recovery. In our consciousness of need we turn to God, petitioning his help. Mrs. Browning puts the matter in a couplet,

> "Lips say, God be pitiful,
> That ne'er say, God be praised!"

In the day of our fullness and satisfaction we do not seek the Lord as in the day of famine and emptiness if our conception of prayer is merely that prayer is a means of getting what we wish for.

Prayer ought to be more than this to every one of us. The prayer which is real is communion with God. It is not only a plea for grace; it is an acknowledgment of grace. It loses itself in the dear sense of the endless love of God as a drop is lost in the brimming cup; as a wave is lost in the sea. Prayer is adoration. It is man lifting his soul to God in rejoicing, and owning that every good gift and every perfect gift comes down from above. They who live near God in daily life must be often with him in prayer, and from the hour of silence in his presence they will never fail to derive refreshment.

Prayer may properly carry every temporal anxiety to the throne of grace and leave it there; for if God so clothe the lilies of the field, as he does in their beautiful raiment, shall he not much more clothe us? But its larger scope, its more insistent meaning, should lead it to convey the desires of the spirit and the soul to him who can make our higher nature regnant over whatever is lower. The disciple will emulate his Master in intercession for those who know not the Lord. Sometimes we exhaust ourselves in endeavors for our children, our friends, for those who have not found Christ precious, but we forget that we may do more for them by talking about them to our Heavenly Father than by talking to them in our own partial and imperfect way.

If we have the right feeling about our relation to this dear Saviour, whose we are, and whom we serve, and are living in an atmosphere of prayer, we shall shrink from no place to which he sends us. He may direct us to the dark cellar and the attic room, to the obscure and the lowly, to the prisoner in his cell, to the untaught and the illiterate. Or he may say to the young Christian girl that he wants her to work for him in society, to shine for him in the drawing-room, to move for him sweet as a flower, harmonious as music, in gay throngs where there are few who love him but many who need him. "I am thine, dear Lord," the child's answer will ring back, in response to the command, and in the white satin and fine linen and purple of social splendor or in the rough homespun of poverty the child will discover the sphere of duty. Each of us in this world following Christ is like the ship which puts out to sea under sealed orders, our duty being just to go where we are sent.

Perhaps you have read the life of Saint

Theresa, whose name is in the Roman calendar,
and who was a Spanish lady abbess of the Six-
teenth Century. She was a woman of deep piety
and unreserved consecration, and her biographer
tells us that she entered wonderfully into the
reality of the Christian life. "Our Lord was as
present, as near and as affable to this extraordinary saint as ever he was to Martha or Mary
Magdalene or the mother of Zebedee's children.
She prepared him where to lay his head. She
sat at his feet and heard his word. She chose
the better part, and he acknowledged to herself
and to others that she had done so. She washed
his feet with her tears and wiped them with the
hair of her head. She had been forgiven much
and she loved much. He said to her, 'Mary,'
and she answered him, 'Rabboni!' And he gave
her messages to his disciples who had not waited
for him as she had waited, till she was able to
say to them all that she had seen the Lord, and
that he had spoken such and such things within
her." One of Theresa's talks about prayer ap-
peals to many readers because of its practical
application to everyday trials and vicissitudes:

"The true proficiency of the soul consists not
so much in deep thinking or eloquent speaking or

beautiful writing as in much and warm loving.
Now if you ask me in what way this much and
warm love may be acquired, I answer, By resolv-
ing to do the will of God and by watching to do
his will as often as occasion offers. Those who
truly love God love all good wherever they find
it. They seek all good to all men. They encourage all good in all men. They commend all
good, they always unite themselves with all
good, they always acknowledge and defend all
good. They have no quarrels. They bear no
envy. O Lord, give me more and more of this
blessed love. Grant me grace not to quit this
underworld life till I no longer desire anything,
nor am capable of loving anything, save thee
alone. Grant that I may use this word 'love'
with regard to thee alone, since there is no solid-
ity for my love to rest on save in thee. The soul
has her own ways of understanding, and of
finding in herself by certain signs and great
conjectures, whether she really loves his Divine
Majesty or no. Her love is full of high impulses, and longings to see and to be with and
to be like God. All else tires and wearies out
the soul. The best of created things disappoint
and torment the soul. God alone satisfies the

soul, till it is impossible to dissemble or mistake such a love. When once I came to see the great beauty of our Lord it turned all other comeliness to corruption to me. My heart could rest on nothing and on no one but himself. When anything else would enter my heart I had only to turn my eyes for a moment in upon that supreme beauty that was engraven within me. So that it is now impossible for any created thing to so possess my soul as not to be instantly expelled, and my mind and heart set free by a little effort to recover the remembrance of the goodness and beauty of our Lord."

This conscious dwelling with Christ should make the disciple a blithe companion on the road. Andrew Bonar of Scotland, a man much in prayer, used to say, "We should always be wearing the garment of praise, not just waving a palm-branch now and then." "Thanksgiving," said the same dear saint, "is the very air of heaven. The oil of joy calms down the waves of trouble." Keble knew the secret of this rare state of mind when he wrote:

"Who but a Christian through all life
    That blessing may prolong,
Who, through the world's sad day of strife,
    Still chants his morning song.

"Ever the richest, tenderest glow
Sets round the autumnal sun.
But there sight fails; no heart may know
The bliss when life is done."

Dr. A. J. Gordon so lived a life hidden with Christ in God that his very countenance shone, and all sorts of men—tramps, drunkards, desperate persons—turned to him with confidence knowing that he would listen to their cry for help, and help them if he could. He knew that "a little talk with Jesus" better than anything else "smooths the rugged way."

Elizabeth Prentiss, wife, mother, author, friend, and as sanctified and set apart as Saint Theresa herself—for let no one think that God especially honors those who from a mistaken desire to please him retreat from the world—during her long and most useful life spent much time in her closet. Prayer was to her the Christian's vital breath, and her letters, her conversations with friends, her whole tenor of living, showed that she was often alone with God. She wrote in her diary, at a time when her health was much impaired:

"Another peaceful, pleasant Sunday, whose only drawback has been the want of strength to

get down on my knees and praise and pray to
my Saviour, as I long to do. For well as I am,
and astonishingly improved in every way, a
very few minutes' use of my voice, even in a
whisper, in prayer, exhausts me to such a degree that I am ready to faint. This seems so
strange when I can go on talking to any extent
—but then it is talking without emotion and in
a desultory way. Ah, well! God knows best in
what manner to let me live; and I desire to ask
for nothing but a docile, acquiescent temper,
whose only petition shall be, 'What wilt thou
have me to do?' not how can I get most enjoyment along the way. I can not believe, if I am
his child, that he will let anything hinder my
progress in the divine life. It seems dreadful
that I have gone on so slowly, and backward so
many times—but then I have been thinking
this is 'to humble and to prove me, and to do me
good in the latter end.' . . . I thank my
God and Saviour for every faint desire he gives
me to see him as he is, and to be changed into
his image, and for every struggle against sin
he enables me to make. It is all of him. I do
wish I loved him better! I do wish he were
never out of my thoughts, and that the aim to

do his will swallowed up all other desires and strivings. Satan whispers that will never be. But it shall be! One day—oh, longed-for, blessed, blissful day!—Christ will become my All in all! Yes, even mine!"

Again, she was writing to a young friend in much trouble of mind concerning his salvation:

"I dare not answer your letter, just received, in my own strength, but must pray over it long. It is a great thing to learn how far our doubts and despondencies are the direct result of physical causes, and another great thing is, when we can not trace any such connection, to bear patiently and quietly what God *permits*, if he does not authorize. I have no more doubt that you love him, and that he loves you, than that I love him and that he loves me. You have been daily in my prayers. Temptations and conflict are inseparable from the Christian life; no strange thing has happened to you. Let me comfort you with the assurance that you will be taught more and more by God's Spirit how to resist; and that true strength and holy manhood will spring up from this painful soil. Try to take heart; there is more than one foot-print on the sands of time to prove that 'some forlorn and shipwrecked brother' has traversed them before you, and come off conqueror through the Beloved. *Don't stop praying, for your life!* Be as cold and emotionless as you please; God will accept your naked faith, when it has no glow or warmth in it; and in his own time the loving, glad heart will come back to you. You can't complain of any folly to which I could not plead guilty. I have put my Saviour's patience to every possible test; and how I love him when I think what he will put up with!

"You ask if I 'ever feel that religion is a sham.' No; never. I *know* it is a reality. If you ask if I am ever staggered by the inconsistencies of professing Christians, I say yes; I am often made heartsick by them; but heartsickness always makes me run to Christ, and one good look at him pacifies me. This is in fact my panacea for every ill; and as to my own sinfulness, that would certainly overwhelm me if I spent much time in looking at it. But it is a monster whose face I do not love to see; I turn from its hideousness to the beauty of his face who sins not, and the sight of 'yon lovely Man' ravishes me. But at your age I did this only by fits and starts, and suffered as you do. So I know how to feel for you, and what to ask for you. God purposely sickens us of man and of self that we may learn to 'look long at Jesus.'"

One test of our discipleship is found, I think, just where Mrs. Prentiss stood when she took time in her busy life to pray for, and to write to, a friend about the interests of the soul. Let us interrogate ourselves concerning our talks with our Father in heaven. Are they altogether self-ish, or are we concerned for those who are without the pale; for those whom we love but who do not love Christ?

Do we ever escape from the group of our own intimate acquaintances and feel a yearning for those whom we do not know, but for whom Christ died?

> "There were ninety and nine that safely lay
> In the shelter of the fold."

They were protected from the storm, but the Shepherd cared for the one that was out in the wilderness, and his voice said,

> "I go to the desert to find my sheep."

The true heroes of Christendom to-day are those men and women who, caring not for ease and scorning luxury, are willing to endure hard-

ship, privation and loneliness, living in remote
fastnesses of the mountains, in Chinese villages,
in Hindu cities, in fishers' huts by the Arabian
Sea, that they may tell the lost of the Saviour.
They could never bear their lives if they were
not often in prayer, if talking with the Heavenly
Father were not their meat and drink.

CHAPTER XXIII

Devout Women of an Elder Day

Star-like in its radiance, the story of Ruth, the fair maiden of Moab who, when her young husband died, clung so loyally to her sorrowful mother-in-law, still beams from the sacred page. Ruth in those old days was as unique as any Enid, Elaine, or Priscilla of a later time.

A certain man of Beth-lehem-judah, by name Elimelech, finding it impossible to care for his family during one of the famines which visited the land, emigrated with them to the country of Moab. We are not to imagine that Elimelech meant to remain in Moab beyond the immediate exigence of the situation. He went to sojourn there, to stay where there was pasture for his flocks and food for his household and where his sons could grow up in comfort, until again the rains should fall and the harvests spring, and his native Beth-lehem be again a house of bread. Sojourn carries in its very meaning and sound a significance which we know when we talk of doing things by the day.

But the little family group was never again to dwell in one home in the dear land where Elimelech had wooed Naomi, in the pleasant land where the true God was worshiped and in all the sanctuary rites there was a foreshadowing of the Lamb slain from the foundation of the world. They continued a long while in Moab, and made friends there, and there Elimelech died, and Naomi was left a widow, with two sons who, after the Oriental fashion, married and brought home their wives, to be to her as daughters. One was Orpah, one was Ruth; and for ten years they dwelt together, when Mahlon and Chilion both died. Then indeed was Naomi left desolate, for in the alien country her roots had not struck deeply, and she turned in her homesick misery to go back to her own people and her father's house.

Nothing can exceed the pathos of the story. Naomi embraced her daughters-in-law, and bade them leave her.

"Wherefore she went forth out of the place where she was, and her two daughters-in-law with her; and they went on the way to return unto the land of Judah. And Naomi said unto her two daughters-in-law, Go, return each to her mother's house: the Lord deal kindly with you, as ye have dealt with the dead, and with me."

But they refused to go, Orpah partially, Ruth absolutely; Orpah went back, gently reluctant, but after all relieved and light of heart, to her own family, her mother, and her gods, to find a husband in Moab, and to be heard of no more forever.

Not so Ruth. She clung to the weeping Naomi, offering her young strength to aid that weakness of oncoming age. In words which, though familiar through much repetition, still drip with sweetness and vibrate with melody she said: "Entreat me not to leave thee, or to return from following after thee: for whither thou goest, I will go; and where thou lodgest, I will lodge: thy people shall be my people, and thy God my God: where thou diest, will I die, and there will I be buried: the Lord do so to me, and more also, if aught but death part thee and me."

Thenceforward the two women walked on together, and came, mother and daughter bound by a new and tender tie, to Beth-lehem. The landscape beckoned Naomi; to Ruth it was the land of exile, bravely chosen and not unwelcome.

She was going with Naomi to Naomi's old
friends and acquaintances, but also to care and
toil and poverty; for Naomi went out full and
was returning empty.

It was the beginning of the barley harvest,
and in those days the rich, according to the
thoughtful consideration of the Mosaic economy,
made a certain provision for the poor by leaving
ears for them to glean in the track of the reapers.
Boaz was a noble and generous citizen of Beth-
lehem, and though not next of kin was of the
family of Elimelech. Naomi sent Ruth to glean
in the rich man's fields; he saw and was at-
tracted by the lovely girl; in due season he married her and thus redeemed the debt which their
kindred owed to those who were gone. Ruth,
thus entering in the Messianic line, became the
grandmother of David and an ancestress of Him
who was the lily of the valley and the rose of
Sharon, the bright and morning star of the
world's darkness, the hope of Israel, the Friend
and Master of the great company of the ransomed. Thus met Gentile with Jew in the lin-
eage of the Christ.

Loyalty, obedience, cheerfulness and faith
seem the distinguishing characteristics of the

beautiful Ruth. A country girl, reared among the mountains and the fields, she brought to the statelier and more luxurious life which was hers as the wife of Boaz the traditions and the strength of the hills. Reared in idolatry, she came out of its fetters into the freedom of the one true worship, into the company of those who adored Jehovah. She forsook her own people and her father's house, and to her was fulfilled in abundant measure the word spoken by the Lord: "Instead of thy fathers shall be thy children, whom thou shalt make princes in all the earth; I will make thy name to be remembered in all generations; therefore shall the peoples give thee thanks forever and ever."

Elizabeth Barrett Browning, describing a beautiful and unselfish woman, said of her, words which might have been applied with equal fitness to Ruth of Moab:

"Her air had a meaning, her movements a grace;
You turned from the fairest to gaze on her face;
And when you had once seen her forehead and mouth
You saw as distinctly her soul and her truth.

"I doubt if she said to you much that could act
As a thought or suggestion; she did not attract
In the sense of the brilliant or wise; I infer
'Twas her thinking of others made you think of her."

Longfellow, in a very familiar lyric, alluded to our heroine thus; it is a lover addressing his beloved:

> "Long was the good man's sermon
>   But it seemed not so to me,
> For he spake of Ruth the beautiful,
>   And then I thought of thee."

As long as time endures, poet and painter will turn wistfully toward the vision of the fair woman gleaning "amid the alien corn," and all generations shall call her blessed.

Many years later the gifted grandson of Ruth already predestined to be king of Israel, with the chrism of Samuel's flask upon his head but in peril of life through the enmity of Saul, was wandering, an outlaw, in the wilderness of Paran. A band of other outlaws, brave, daring, and adventurous, the Robin Hoods of the period, surrounded their splendid young captain and did his bidding. In Carmel, near the forests where David and his men found shelter, there was a rich and very great man who had flocks and herds. There are men to-day who count their wealth by many figures, and who are as sordid of heart and as truly paupers in spirit as was Nabal the churl. He had three thousand sheep and a thousand goats and the annual sheep shearing had come, and a very natural request was sent to the owner of these vast flocks by the soldier, who for many months had not only refrained from molesting the shepherds of Nabal but had with a strong hand kept other marauders away. The Bible narrative is Homeric in its simplicity:

"And David heard in the wilderness that Nabal did shear his sheep. And David sent out ten young men, and David said unto the young men, Get you up to Carmel, and go to Nabal, and greet him in my name: and thus shall ye say to him that liveth in prosperity, Peace be both to thee, and peace be to thine house, and peace be unto all that thou hast. And now I have heard that thou hast shearers: now thy shepherds which were with us, we hurt them not, neither was there aught missing unto them, all the while they were in Carmel. Ask thy young men, and they will shew thee. Wherefore let the young men find favour in thine eyes; for we come in a good day: give, I pray thee, whatsoever cometh to thine hand unto thy servants, and to thy son David. And when David's young men came, they spake to Nabal according to all

those words in the name of David, and ceased.
And Nabal answered David's servants, and said,
Who is David? and who is the son of Jesse?
there be many servants nowadays that break
away every man from his master. Shall I then
take my bread, and my water, and my flesh that
I have killed for my shearers, and give it unto
men, whom I know not whence they be? So
David's young men turned their way, and went
again, and came and told him all those sayings.
And David said unto his men, Gird ye on every
man his sword. And they girded on every man
his sword; and David also girded on his sword:
and there went up after David about four hundred men; and two hundred abode by the stuff.
But one of the young men told Abigail, Nabal's
wife, saying, Behold, David sent messengers out
of the wilderness to salute our master; and he
railed on them. But the men were very good
unto us, and we were not hurt, neither missed
we any thing, as long as we were conversant with
them, when we were in the fields. They were a
wall unto us both by night and day, all the while
we were with them keeping the sheep. Now
therefore know and consider what thou wilt do,
for evil is determined against our master and

against all his house, for he is such a son of Belial that one cannot speak to him."

Abigail, Nabal's wife, was a comely matron of rare understanding, the type of the prudent housewife, a great lady, with a heart and brain which rose to meet the occasion. David was riding rapidly towards her home, with four hundred fierce and angry armed men; such an armament as might well cause terror to spring in the breasts of those against whom its attack was presently to be made. They were famished men too, gaunt with hunger, and sterner for privation and disappointment; reckless, and justly resentful at ingratitude and insult. According to the canons of their day, they were fully within their right in visiting a swift and utter wreck on Nabal and his house. Indeed, in the war canons of any day, hatred, malice, wrath and cruelty stalk unrebuked, and David's intended onslaught on Nabal is not without its parallels in our nineteenth century.

Abigail, wise woman that she was, lost no time. The men must be conciliated. They were starving and must be appeased by food. Hastily she gathered such provision as in a well appointed household was at her hand.

"Then Abigail made haste and took two hundred loaves, and two bottles of wine, and five sheep ready dressed, and five measures of parched corn, and an hundred clusters of raisins, and two hundred cakes of figs, and laid them on asses. And she said unto her young men, Go on before me; behold, I come after you. But she told not her husband Nabal. And it was so, as she rode on her ass, and came down by the covert of the mountain, that, behold, David and his men came down against her; and she met them. Now David had said, Surely in vain have I kept all that this fellow hath in the wilderness, so that nothing was missed of all that pertained unto him: and he hath returned me evil for good. God do so unto the enemies of David, and more also, if I leave of all that pertain to him by the morning light so much as one man child. And when Abigail saw David, she hasted, and lighted off her ass, and fell before David on her face, and bowed herself to the ground. And she fell at his feet, and said, Upon me, my lord, upon me be the iniquity: and let thine handmaid, I pray thee, speak in thine ears, and hear thou the words of thine handmaid. Let not my Lord, I

pray thee, regard this man of Belial, even
Nabal: for as his name is, so is he; Nabal is his
name, and folly is with him: but I thine handmaid saw not the young men of my lord, whom
thou didst send. Now therefore, my lord, as the
Lord liveth, and as thy soul liveth, seeing the
Lord hath withholden thee from bloodguiltiness,
and from avenging thyself with thine own hand,
now therefore let thine enemies, and them that
seek evil to my lord, be as Nabal. And now this
present which thy servant hath brought unto
my lord, let it be given unto the young men that
follow my lord. Forgive, I pray thee, the tres-
pass of thine handmaid: for the Lord will certainly make my lord a sure house, because my
lord fighteth the battles of the Lord; and evil
shall not be found in thee all thy days. And
though man be risen up to pursue thee, and to
seek thy soul, yet the soul of my lord shall be
bound in the bundle of life with the Lord thy
God; and the souls of thine enemies, them shall
he sling out, as from the hollow of a sling. And
it shall come to pass, when the Lord shall have
done to my lord according to all the good that
he hath spoken concerning thee, and shall have
appointed thee prince over Israel; that this shall

be no grief unto thee, nor offence of heart unto
my lord, either that thou hast shed blood cause-
less, or that my lord hath avenged himself: and
when the Lord shall have dealt well with my
lord, then remember thine handmaid. And
David said to Abigail, Blessed be the Lord, the
God of Israel, which sent thee this day to meet
me: and blessed be thy wisdom, and blessed be
thou, which hast kept me this day from bloodguiltiness, and from avenging myself with mine
own hand. For in very deed, as the Lord, the
God of Israel, liveth, which hath withholden me
from hurting thee, except thou hadst hasted and
come to meet me, surely there had not been left
unto Nabal by the morning light so much as one
man child. So David received of her hand that
which she had brought him: and he said unto
her, Go up in peace to thine house; see, I have
hearkened to thy voice, and have accepted thy
person."

We may note the exceeding tact of Abigail in
her approach to David, in her choice of a gift to
be sent on before her, and in her appeal to his
higher nature. When the days of his obscurity
and peril should have passed, and the Lord
should have brought him unto honor and do-

minion, she told him it would be a grief of heart to remember having needlessly shed innocent blood. Her wit, discretion and good sense prevailed, and David withheld his men from violence and left Nabal's estate in peace. Nabal indeed died soon after, but it was at the hand of the Lord and not by the weapons of David.

Abigail's portrait might well have been in Solomon's mind when he drew the model woman in matchless lines:

"Who can find a virtuous woman? for her price is far above rubies. The heart of her husband doth safely trust in her, so that he shall have no need of spoil. She will do him good and not evil all the days of her life. . . . She looketh well to the ways of her household and eateth not the bread of idleness."

We do not know the name of the Queen of Sheba, but she had courage, and curiosity, and a desire to learn more than she could in her own land, and so, when rumors were brought to her of a young monarch who was wise and masterful, and possessed of the favor of the Most High, she came with a very great train—camels that bare spices and gold in abundance and precious stones. One can see the grand lady in her litter,

her guards around her, her soldiers riding in
front and rear, and far behind her; the ships of
the desert slowly passing with their freight of
the precious and the rare. We have only a
glimpse of her as she is entertained by King
Solomon, and we can picture her surprise and
pleasure as she finds that the half has not been
told her of the state and splendor which surrounded him. No doubt she carried back new
ideas to her people and her friends, and a glim-
mering of the light which was yet to lighten the
world.

Esther, the Jewish girl who was elevated to
the throne of Persia, divides with Ruth the interest of Bible readers, since she too was young
and fair, and since in immortal youth and
beauty she moves through the course of history.
Ahasuerus has little to commend him to our
admiration. This proud, petulant, arrogant
and despotic sovereign first deeply insulted his
wife, Queen Vashti, and then childishly deposed
her from her position. A succession of young
women were inspected, as slaves in the market
might be, before one was found who in all re-
spects pleased the royal tyrant. One pities
Esther even when she obtained grace and favor

in the sight of the king, and when he loved her
above all the women. No love, as we know that
pure and hallowed passion, could exist in the
breast of a polygamous Eastern king. Esther
simply entered the harem as chief favorite, with
the distinction of being the king's wife and perhaps the mother of his heir. It may be that
Vashti was childless, in which case she would
have lost one of her strongest holds on the husband who paid her so little respect.

We know the story—how Haman plotted to
destroy the Jews by wholesale, then as now the
Hebrews, by reason of sagacity, thrift and supreme cleverness, being objects of envy to other
and less gifted nations; and how Mordecai discovered and defeated the wicked conspiracy,
aided by Esther, who alone could help her people in the crisis. Her "If I perish, I perish," as
she waits for the king to extend the golden scepter, still touches our hearts.

Not so, dear friends, need we approach the
presence chamber of our gracious Lord and
King. He is ever extending the scepter of his
merciful favor, and when we will we may go to
him, sure of an audience, and sure of a reception
full of kindness and compassion.

No one who has with care perused the Old
Testament narratives has failed to observe the
recognition given to motherhood. The mothers
made the men, then as now, and if a king were
good or were bad, were reverent or profane, one
had not to look very far to see what sort of
mother brought him up.

16   229

CHAPTER XXIV

DAILY PROBLEMS

IN THE MORNING

HERE'S a new day; blessed Jesus,
   Wilt thou take it for thine own?
In its hours may I serve thee,
   Looking ever to the throne.

Keep me in the strong temptation
   That I may not fall away,
Be thy love my full salvation
   From Satanic wiles to-day.

Hold me safe in sudden trial,
   Let me know thy presence near;
Give me gràce for self-denial,
   Present blessing, Saviour dear.

If this day an earthly friendship
   Fail me like the smoking flax,
Let my hold on thee be firmer,
   Nor my grasp of heaven relax.

Wholly thine, my blessed Master,
   Wholly thine, in work or rest,
This day, all days, till the last one
   When I lean me on thy breast.

I was present the other day when several
young people were discussing the character of
a relative slightly known to me, and just then

an object of sympathy because she had lost her home.

"I don't know what will become of her," said Katharine. "Cousin Dorinda is a good woman, nobody can doubt her piety, but she is very hard to live with. Somehow, she never fits in anywhere. Where another person would conciliate she antagonizes, and a spirit of contention follows wherever she goes."

Her own sister said: "If Dorinda is to come here I might as well break up housekeeping at once. She would ruin the peace of our home."

Louise took up the conversation. "Yes," she said, thoughtfully, "I know. Cousin Dorinda is very sensitive. If she cannot have her own way she either goes about looking black and sullen like a thunder cloud, making everybody wretched, or else she melts into tears, and cries and puts the family in the wrong. Nobody has ever had patience with her except grandmother, and now that she is gone nobody on this earth wants Dorinda. She is simply an impossible person in a household. She is, as Katharine says, 'hard to live with.'"

My thoughts went very sorrowfully toward this absent Dorinda, whose disposition was so unfortunate. Our mothers do bear with us when the rest of the world refuses its tolerance, and hers had apparently borne with her. But the patient mother heart was no longer here, and friends and kith and kin were all afraid of the constant companionship of Dorinda. She was not rich enough to live by herself in independence, nor strong enough to go out in the business world and find employment by which she could earn her bread. A good housekeeper, a lady by birth and training, a member of the church, and, I am sure, a sincere disciple of Christ, Dorinda, at forty-five, was desired nowhere, because of her "contrary ways." In those two words a nephew summed up his opinion of the aunt whom he emphatically hoped would not take up her abode under his roof. She was a woman of *contrary* ways.

Thinking it over, it came to me that Dorinda had been making herself an unpopular and un-desired member of society by slow degrees, and during a term of years. As a child and a young girl she had been a little willful, perhaps, and perhaps a trifle too pronounced in her manner of stating a position and holding up her end of an argument. Gradually, a little at a time, her peculiarities had become intensified. She had allowed her temper to triumph over politeness and kindness. She had lost self-control. She had grown difficult; a person to be studied; a person of moods and caprices, a person unloving, I am afraid, and whom people did not love.

If I were writing about the duties of others to Dorinda I would drop a hint that it would be well to exercise gentleness to a woman in her case, to be specially tender and considerate, as one would be to an invalid or a crippled person, since here was a calamity, not to the body, but to the heart and mind. I did not feel that Louise and Katharine and the young nephew were wholly in the right, as I observed how lacking in charity they were to their kinswoman. But I am not writing for them to-day, and so I will just quote a favorite Scripture text and pass on to my subject: "We that are strong ought to bear the infirmities of the weak." Even infirmities like those of a cross, resentful, and annoying person in the family may be borne with serenity by those who are strong and recruit their strength daily by prayer to Christ.

But does it ever appeal to you, dear young girl, to you, Marjorie or Dorothy, that a time may come when your acquaintances may speak of you pityingly, as one who has ways, and moods, and who is not easy to get on with? How would you like it, if, having grown older, you should observe that younger people were shy of being their real selves in your company? That they repressed speech, and studied your expression, and were afraid to be mirthful if you were in the room? Every middle-aged or elderly woman or man who has ever had this humiliating experience was once young; and there was a beginning, when faults which are now blots upon his or her individuality were so small that no one suspected their existence.

The lesson for us, every one, is to be watchful of our manner; watchful of our words. We should daily seek to grow in unselfishness and in likeness to the Saviour. Few of us will ever have the opportunity to perform great deeds of heroism, but to every one of us there is given the chance day by day to be sweet and gracious and winsome. No one who reads this need ever become, like poor Miss Dorinda, a dread to her friends and family if only she will begin now to cultivate the art of responsive kindness; if she will determine to be easy, not hard, to live with.

From living together in the home the transition is easy to living together in the church and in the community. We cannot separate ourselves from the people next door, nor from the acquaintances over the way, nor from the friends in the opposite pew. It still exists, though if we form our conclusions from observations taken in our great bustling cities we shall be quite ready to affirm that neighborliness is a thing of the past. One is more and more struck with the unfriendliness of a great town. You do not know—often you do not care to know—the people who live next door to you on either side, and the dwellers on the opposite corner or at the other end of the street are as remote from your consciousness as if they lived in Patagonia. It happens not infrequently that you grow accustomed to certain familiar figures: an old gentleman with a gold-headed cane; a lady who wears the dignity of her eighty years as she does her satin cloak and velvet bonnet. After a while these persons cease to be denizens of the street. They have grown feeble and are remaining indoors, or they have faded out of life. The brisk business man who goes at the same hour each morning to his office or shop, who catches a certain car at the corner, becomes known to you as a resident in the vicinity, but you have no particular curiosity about his name or circumstances.

One day you go home from a round of visits, or from your own business office, and you see a wreath of flowers on the door-bell of the neighboring house, and people going in and out, and you are aware that that gray and shadowy angel, who impartially visits every home in the world when its turn comes, has crossed your neighbor's threshold. But it is nothing to you. Possibly you inquire the circumstances; very likely you remind yourself that you did not know the person in life, and that you have no right to intrude with inquiries or sympathy upon the survivors—who have their own friends and do not need you.

If you have had your early home in a sociable, friendly village where everybody knew everybody else, where it was the custom to hob-nob over the garden gate with the man next door—where the whole town rejoiced when some great honor or happiness came to a child of the place and the whole town grieved when there was a corresponding sorrow—you feel very lonesome and desolate in your first plunge into city life.

Do not, however, forget that in our country there are many phases of life; and that while a nomad instinct has brought many wayfarers to the city, to find the solitude of crowds, yet there still are joy and love and friendliness in many smaller towns and villages and along the pleasant country-side. It still happens that a neighbor in one of these blessed smaller places, finding herself suddenly able to take a week's journey with her husband, may call upon her friend next door to mother her brood while she is gone. Not long ago, in a lovely Southern town where I was visiting, I called upon a beautiful and childless woman whose charming home was at the moment fairly overflowing with juvenile life. Little white-haired boys and girls were playing on the veranda with their dolls and little carts, a motherly black nurse sat on the door-step with a dimpled baby in her arms, and my friend observed: "My neighbor has gone to California and I am taking care of her children for her until she returns." Could sisterly kindness go farther than this? For the friends were simply friends—not relatives—and this kind neighbor was taking on herself the responsibility of looking after the possible accidents which might befall a flock of restless boys, the possible croups and fevers which might attack the little ones in the night, while the mother went happily away on her journey without a care; knowing how safe her children would be in the hands of her friend.

In the same city, if company unexpectedly arrives and the dessert is not sufficient, near neighbors are quite willing to go without theirs that the friend whose guests have come may not find herself at a loss. Pies and puddings, creams and custards, are sent over the back fence; and in one instance, when a husband unexpectedly brought home with him three old college-mates who had dropped in upon him from space, his wife, knowing that the modest steak provided for dinner would not satisfy these hungry appetites, went confidently to her neighbor next door. An exchange was presently effected, and a goodly roast smoking from the oven made its appearance on the table where it was needed, while the steak changed hands and sufficed for the wants of the family who had no company. This kind of pleasant, unofficial neighborliness has not departed from a thousand of our Southern towns, from our New England villages, and

from our blessed country homes in any part of
the land.

In our cities we have many advantages; as,
for example, the trained nurse, who comes at
a moment's call in the hour of calamity or anxiety or of severe illness, but in country places
where the trained nurse is not easily attainable
there are yet to be found kind and motherly
women with faculty, women who understand
nursing, and who come to a household in its
hour of extremity and do their womanly best.
"My husband lay at death's door for weeks," said
a friend to me. "I don't know what I should
have done if my neighbors had not taken turns
in helping me care for him." Thinking of in-
stances like this one repeats the old Bible phrase
with thankfulness, "Better is a neighbor that is
near than a brother that is far off."

I question if we do not lose a great deal by
limiting our neighborly acquaintance and our
neighborly interchange of kindness as we do in
our town life. Many a time there is an aching
heart not far off which we may cheer. Often,
if we would encourage the impulse, we might become pleasantly acquainted with people divided
from us only by a narrow partition wall, and it

would do us good and not evil to come in touch
with their lives. There is a certain sadness in
the thought that we sometimes miss an acquaintance and after a little interval of days or weeks
inquire what has become of her, and are told
that she was buried at such a time. We might
at least have gone to take a look at the still face
or laid a flower upon the coffin. That act of
kindness would not have hurt us, and it might
have been balm and sweetness to some wounded
and mourning heart.

INDOORS AT NIGHT

Keen and cold is the wintry blast
As the sleet and snow go driving past;
There's a strife in the old trees, racked and bent,
The clouds hang low o'er the firmament,
But the household gathers safe and warm,
Folded close from the freezing storm;
The lamp is lighted, the hearth is bright,
And the dear ones are cozy indoors at night.

And when shutters are closed and curtains drawn,
And the toiling hours of the day are gone,
Sweet words are spoken, good nights are said
To the wee ones tucked in the little bed.
(God's grace watch over each curly head!)
Then with book, and talk, and the dear old song
We have loved since the days when we were young,
We will fill the hours with love's delight,
Cozy and happy indoors at night.

Trustful To-morrows

Trust

I know not if to-morrow
  Shall bless me like to-day;
Of night I sometimes borrow
  Dark clouds and shadows gray;
For sinful, sick and weary,
  Of this I still am sure:
No clouds or shadows dreary
  Shall my sweet heaven obscure.

Oh, much is left uncertain
  In this strange life below;
But faith lifts up the curtain
  And sees the inner glow;
And nothing now can move me,
  Nor shake my joy so pure;
For Christ has stooped to love me,
  And of his love I'm sure.

If the Lord Should Come

If the Lord should come in the morning
  As I went about my work—
The little things and the quiet things
  That a servant cannot shirk,
Though nobody ever sees them,
  And only the dear Lord cares
That they always are done in the light of the sun—
  Would he take me unawares?

If my Lord should come at noonday,
  The time of the dust and heat,
When the glare is white, and the air is still,
  And the hoof-beats sound in the street—
If my dear Lord came at noonday,
  And smiled in my tired eyes,
Would it not be sweet his look to meet?
  Would he take me by surprise?

If my Lord came hither at evening,
  In the fragrant dew and dusk,
When the world drops off its mantle
  Of daylight like a husk
And flowers in wonderful beauty,
  And we fold our hands and rest,
Would his touch of my hand, his low command,
  Bring me unhoped-for zest?

Why do I ask and question?
  He is ever coming to me,
Morning and noon and evening,
  If I have but eyes to see.
And the daily load grows lighter,
  The daily cares grow sweet,
For the Master is near, the Master is here,
  I have only to sit at his feet.

GOOD INTENTIONS

What wonderful things we have planned, Love,
  What beautiful things we have done,
What fields we have tilled, what gifts we have willed,
  In the light of another year's sun!
When we think of it all we are baffled,
  There's so much that never comes true;
Because, Love, instead of our doing,
  We're always just meaning to do.

The friends we are wanting to help, Love,
  They struggle alone and forlorn,
By trial and suffering vanquished,
  Perchance by temptation o'erborne:
But the lift, and the touch, and the greeting
  That well might have aided them through
The perilous strait of ill-fortune,
  They miss: we're but meaning to do.

Trustful To-morrows

We dream of a fountain of knowledge;
  We loiter along on its brink,
And toy with the crystalline waters,
  Forever just meaning to drink.
Night falls, and our tasks are unfinished,
  Too late our lost chances we rue,
Dear Love, while our comrades were doing
  We only were MEANING TO DO.

Betake Thyself to Prayer

When bitter winds of trouble blow,
And thou art tossing to and fro,
When waves are rolling mountain high,
And clouds obscure the steadfast sky,
Fear not, my soul; thy Lord is there,
Betake thyself, my soul, to prayer.

When in the dull routine of life
Thou yearnest half for pain and strife,
So weary of the commonplace,
Of days that wear the self-same face,
Think softly, soul; thy Lord is there.
And then betake thyself to prayer.

When brims thy cup with sparkling joy,
When happy tasks the hours employ,
When men with praise and sweet acclaim
Upon the highway speak thy name,
Then, soul, I bid thee have a care;
Seek oft thy Lord in fervent prayer.

If standing where two pathways meet,
Each beckoning thy pilgrim feet,
Thou art in doubt which road to take,
Look up, and say: "For thy dear sake—
O Master! show thy footprints fair—
I'd follow thee." Christ answers prayer.

The tempter oft, with wily toil,
Seeks thee, my soul, as precious spoil;
His weapons never lose their edge,
But thou art Heaven's peculiar pledge.
Though Satan rage, thy Lord is there—
Dear soul, betake thyself to prayer.

CHAPTER XXV

With Level Eyes

"I had never realized my mother as an individual," said a grown daughter, "until she came to visit our college at commencement. To me she had always been just 'mother'—the dearest, best, most tender and considerate of mothers; but I never compared her with any one, or saw her as she was to others, or thought of her as a noble woman, able to hold her own anywhere, till I looked at her away from her own background. At last I saw her with level eyes, and I was proud of my mother."

To the mother it comes almost with a shock, that her daughter, the little girl whom she cradled in her arms, whose little frocks she sat up at night to finish, whose goings to and fro she ordained, who was hers to rule and to guide, has become a personality, herself grown up. When the daughter abides in the household, slipping by unmarked stages from childhood into youth, from youth into maturity, the older woman often fails to notice that the younger has emerged from the period of pupilage and restraint, and too long holds fast to the reins of authority which should not be held over one whose responsibilities are those of the adult human being. We often meet undeveloped daughters even in this period of assertive womanhood; daughters who dwell in their fathers' houses with little freedom of action, with no private purse, and with the coercion of child life, long after the sweetness and the dependence of childish days are over.

I have known women whose faces bore telltale lines of discontent, whose brown hair began to show threads of silver, and who chafed under their lack of personal freedom, yet felt entirely helpless to change the aspect of affairs. Their mothers had never discovered that the children were grown up. They still exacted the peculiar deference and obedience due from a child under tutors and governors to those who bore rule over him or her. A daughter might be forty, but she could not go on a visit, or buy a new gown, or join a class or a club, or do anything, small or great, without asking and obtaining her mother's consent.

At a glance one sees how limiting and dwarfing such a condition must be. Of necessity, and for love's sake, daughters must always be deferential to mothers, but there comes a day when they must stand on their own feet and answer for their own actions. Married, they at once take this independent place in the world; so that a bride of eighteen may have more actual freedom than a spinster of thirty. But when a woman is grown up, whether single or married, she is entitled to the privileges of her age. And if parents are wise, and can possibly afford it, they will secure to the daughter at home, not self-supporting and living under their roof, enough money regularly given, as an allowance, to keep her from feeling like a mendicant or a pauper. If they cannot do this, and the daughter desires it, they should interpose no objection to her going out from home to engage in whatever employment she is best fitted for or for which she can most readily receive training.

When our daughters front us "with level eyes" something beyond motherhood and childhood enters into the relation. A higher friendship, a fuller sympathy, a dearer bond may come with the years, and, being possible, should cer-

tainly come to pass in great sweetness and
strength.

We live in a period of which a certain marked
unrest on the part of our young women is a significant feature. Girlhood has been said by a
thoughtful observer to be not altogether a happy
time of life, though it is so happy-looking. To
whatever cause it may be due, economic or otherwise, whether owing to the richer intellectual
culture or to the growing independence of the
sex, or the greater need of money and the mul-
tiplied doors of occupation in professional and
business life swinging open at a woman's touch,
the fact is patent that home no longer attracts
our girls as it once did. They are apt to look
farther afield for their work. Many of them are
eager to try their powers in the market-place;
many of them have aspirations and ambitions
which domesticity does not wholly satisfy.

Our girls are not to be blamed for this condition of things, which is perhaps only a temporary phase and the sign of a transitional
epoch. But I would ask the educated and earnest young woman of the day to weigh carefully
the opportunities, privileges and obligations
which the home and family offer, before she de-

cides that there is a worthier sphere than this
for the Christian woman. I believe profoundly
that a happy marriage is the most blessed state
into which woman can be called. I regard
honored motherhood as the most queenly position in the earth to-day. If a good man loves a
girl, and she consents to marry him, she will
enter, however poor the two may be, however
they may have to struggle, on a career far more
useful and satisfying than any open to her as a
wage-earner or a worker. Let the Christian
woman illustrate in her home life the beauty of
holiness.

The mother has the first beginnings of life,
the molding and the guiding of childhood. The
Christian mother can hardly help bringing her
little ones to Christ.

Daughters and sisters should show loving attention to father and brothers in the home, and
there comes a day when mothers are tired, or
perhaps ill, and they, too, need sorely the tender
and patient ministry of the young lives which
but lately were dependent on their care. To
Christian daughters I would say, "Be loving
and sweet to your mothers."

The other day, as I sat by my window, I was

the observer of a little incident which set in motion the train of thought reaching from my quiet home to you, wherever you are. I live on a street which has a smooth asphalt pavement greatly in favor with wheelmen and women, and there are few hours between morning and bedtime when young people are not flying up and down its lengths on their magical machines.

A very pretty girl came sweeping along, managing her bicycle with the graceful ease of a confident and skillful rider. Her face was glowing with health, her dress was most becoming, and her whole air was that of one accustomed to the courtesies of polite society, and used, on her own part, to much gentleness and consideration. Yet, when another girl, evidently a novice, swerved awkwardly and narrowly escaped colliding with her, the pretty young woman shocked and amazed the observer in the shadow of the curtains by exclaiming, angrily, "Great Scott! I wish you would look where you are going!"

There was a bit of wholly unconscious revelation of character. I saw that my beautiful maiden was not like the king's daughter, "all glorious within." She had caught, perhaps from a schoolboy brother, the trick of slang; she was impatient, she was hasty of speech and temper, and she failed to make allowance for the inexperience of another. I was saddened, and I wished with my whole heart that the young girl could realize how unfortunate for herself was the frame of mind and the habit of petulance which had made possible her impetuous remonstrance. Life may discipline her by greater trials than the clumsy blunder of a fellow traveler on the road, and by and by she may learn to repress the vehement word of irritation. But what I long for, when I think of her, and of thousands like her, is that they may not feel the impulse to hasty vexation with the errors or even with the carelessness of others. It is a noble thing so to live that the face, manner, voice, and what the Bible aptly terms "walk and conversation," are the expressions of inward poise, serenity and sweetness.

"Such a one does not love her sister," said a friend not long ago, coming from a home where an invalid had been lying at death's door for weeks.

"Why do you think so?" was the inquiry, a very natural one in the circumstances.

"I notice," the reply came slowly, "that she has nothing to say of Jean's sufferings, or of Jean's marvelous patience and fortitude; that she is only impressed with Jean's occasional forgetfulness to thank her for a kindness, and that she dwells mainly on her own fatigue, and the number of invitations she has had to decline owing to this ill-timed illness on Jean's part. Love suffereth long, and is kind; love vaunteth not itself, is not easily provoked; therefore, love would lead the sister who is well to take a different tone about the sister who is laid aside on a bed of pain."

"She would disclaim any lack of affection," said the other; "and there is the excuse for her, too, that she has had a long strain, and is tired."

"That last I grant; nevertheless, whether she is or is not aware of it, she is not in love with Jean. The revelation on her part is entirely unconscious; but it is a plain revelation."

Perhaps you have often heard people say that what one is is of more consequence than what one does, and you have fancied the saying rather trite. It is, however, profoundly true. One who goes on his way living the Christ-life, brave, honest, fearless, unselfish and magnanimous, wins others to the Christ because he shows **forth** the spirit of the Master. One who has not kept his soul a spotless chamber for the indwelling Christ will constantly reveal, when he does not dream it, the insincerity of his professions. We must be good if we would do good. We must reveal ourselves in a thousand ways, whether we mean to or not; and if Christ be in us, as the lamp that guides, we shall reveal Christ.

253

CHAPTER XXVI

Young Women and Self-support

All thoughtful observers must be aware of a significant change in the point of view as regards the relations of young women to the everyday world. In my girlhood it was not customary for the daughters of well-to-do men to engage in work outside the doors of their homes. A man took it for granted that his boys should study for a profession, acquire a trade, or enter upon business life. "John Smith & Sons" was in the anticipated order of things. There is an old and well-known house on Broadway, New York, to-day, of which the style is "John So-and-So, Sons & Sons." This is really a survival of what was formerly the almost invariable routine. A man did not expect his girls to become bread-winners while he was alive to earn their bread, and people would have been rather shocked in that conservative time at the idea of Mary's becoming a reporter, Charlotte a saleswoman, Matilda a nurse, Rebecca a visiting housekeeper. The young ladies helped their mother at home, did a good deal of nursing when any one was ill, were kind and neighborly, made their own frocks on occasion, shopped, visited, were sheltered, protected, and regarded as ornaments to the family circle. Sometimes a girl taught; once in a while one wrote and had poems and stories published, but rather under the rose. It was not a thing to be bruited about in common talk, nor proclaimed from the housetops. Generally girls married in the later teens, or the early twenties, and one who did not marry before twenty-six was, poor child, called rather pityingly an old maid, and had a sort of nimbus of commiseration around her head until she was forty, when her spinsterhood was taken as a matter of course, and, unless she wedded a widower with a large family of growing children, she became the unofficial aunt at large of the whole community.

We used to hear of failures in business which were openly attributed to the extravagance of Brown's wife and daughters. Poor man! he had to pay for their dresses and diamonds, their carriage and horses, and he went under. Have you noticed that one does not often hear such a misfortune in these days thus accounted for? A man comes to wreck in the business world of this period because of too little capital, or too much expansion, or too great competition, or too entire trust in the honesty of others; not because he has a train of women tugging at his heels and clamoring for gewgaws and furbelows. The point of view has entirely changed.

It was once a very common thing to be told that a man had remained a bachelor for the reason—accepted as a valid one by his friends and society—that he had sisters whom he must support. Poor Dennis could not afford to choose a wife—there were Charlotte and Clarrissa who were unmarried, and for them he must provide life's bread and butter every day and life's pot of honey when he could. And people thought this as it should be. A man, of course, was bound to provide for his female relatives. That they should be sent out to battle with the world did not accord with conventional ideas of propriety.

The Civil War, among its other upheavals, brought about the first radical change in this state of things. So many men died in battle or in hospital, so many men came home crippled or permanently disabled, that women, thrust from the nest, were forced to enter fields hitherto pre-empted by men. Widows and orphans found that clerkships could be filled by them as by their husbands, fathers and brothers in the past. A study of statistics shows how sweeping and remarkable and rapid a change in the labor market was due to the Civil War.

Then, closely following this epoch, came the beginning of what we loosely call the higher education of women. The entrance of women on the business world speedily made evident the fact that a different sort of training was needed from that given in the excellent academies and schools from which refined, sweet and capable women had hitherto emerged. Colleges for women must exist, with curriculums as comprehensive and examinations as rigid as those belonging to colleges for men.

The second generation of women graduates will soon be fairly launched upon our country and ready to take a hand in its affairs. Our girls of to-day, whether their fathers be rich or poor, are, almost universally, eagerly reaching forward to careers. They scorn dependence. Far from accepting what parents are often anxious to give, many girls are restless and unhappy unless or until they can secure a place where they may test their powers, show their mettle, and earn and keep a foothold for themselves.

One cannot but at times regret that the pendulum has swung so very far in the other direction, so that to-day comparatively few young women, let their circumstances be easy or the reverse, are contented to settle down and become that beautiful and attractive personage, the daughter of the home. One feels a certain sympathy with fathers and mothers growing old, and longing for the companionship of youth in the family, when one observes how very generally the girl, leaving school and college, finds the domestic routine wearisome, and looks about her for any outside work which may come to her hand. "I have no need to support myself, and no special talent for one thing more than another," said a girl the other day, "but I simply cannot go back to the little dead and alive village where I spent my childhood and vegetate there as my mother has done all her life." I cannot but believe that there is something at fault in the education which suffers young women to keep in lines so narrow, which allows them to be so frankly self-considerate, and which fails to

show them that there is nowhere in the land the
sphere so obscure and so limited that a Christian
woman may not there let her light shine.

The army of poor girls, girls who must earn
their living or be paupers, is so large, and its
needs are so imperative, that rich girls, by whom
I mean all girls who have no necessity to be self-
supporting, should think most seriously before
they increase the pressure on the labor market.
This remark applies particularly to such girls
as the one whose declaration I have just quoted;
for genius is a law unto itself, and a recognized
vocation should be respected, if it be for science,
art, or any department of human effort. Philanthropy has so many openings for well-to-do
girls. Broadly speaking, however, rich girls
should not crowd their poorer sisters to the wall
unless they are very sure that the highest duty
requires it; a call higher than caprice or the desire to be independent, the real call of **duty**,
"stern daughter of the voice of God."

The old complaint that men are more highly
paid than women for services of the same character is largely modified in our period. The
labor organizations have protective legislation
for women on this very subject, and the profes-

sional woman, if able and successful, is paid for her work according to its value, and no discount is made for sex. The vast volume of women pressing into stenography and typewriting, and into shops, may help to cut down the general rate of salaries, but there is not now the unfair discrimination in favor of men which was once a crying evil. One poorly-paid profession, that of teaching, never estimated at its true worth when the matter is of salary, still holds to old standards, and a man devoting his time and talents to teaching receives more money at the end of his term than a woman can command for equal service rendered. But the conditions of the labor market are much more just, so far as women are in concern, than they used to be. Also, the standard is higher, and a woman is more rigidly held to the best possible work than in the past.

Our self-supporting girls are, in the cities, learning to create households of their own; a half dozen artists, journalists, students of music or business women combine their means, rent a small apartment, secure an elder sister or a mother as their chaperone, engage a maid, and live so cosily and charmingly that the thought

of marriage and a home of their individual own
is much less attractive than it might be if they
lived solitary lives in uncomfortable boarding
houses. This is, perhaps, not to be regretted;
since marriage, for any reason except the com-
pelling reason of sincere and uncalculating love,
is very undesirable and something less than
sacred, and should not be entered upon by
woman or man. Still, one notes, as indicative
of the temper of the hour, a growing indifference
to marriage on the part of our educated young
people.

When the march begins in the morning,
   And the heart and the foot are light;
When the flags are all a-flutter,
   And the world is gay and bright;

When the bugles lead the column,
   And the drums are proud in the van,
It's shoulder to shoulder, forward, march!
   Ah! let him lag who can!

For it's easy to march to music
   With your comrades all in line,
And you don't get tired, you feel inspired,
   And life is a draught divine.

When the march drags on at evening
   And the color-bearer's gone;
When the merry strains are silent
   That piped so brave in the dawn;

When you miss the dear old fellows
  Who started out with you;
When it's stubborn and sturdy, forward, march!
  Though the ragged lines are few;

Then it's hard to march in silence,
  And the road has lonesome grown,
And life is a bitter cup to drink,
  But the soldier must not moan.

And this is the task before us,
  A task we may never shirk;
In the gay time and the sorrowful time
  We must march and do our work.

We must march when the music cheers us,
  March when the strains are dumb,
Plucky and valiant, forward, march!
  And smile, whatever may come.

For, whether life's hard or easy,
  The strong man keeps the pace;
For the desolate march and the silent
  The strong soul finds the grace.

CHAPTER XXVII

Counting the Blessings

Because our griefs and cares loom large upon the horizon of our life they are apt to overcloud our sky and cover our pathway with darkness. It is a good plan when tempted to depression to count our blessings. Even the griefs may be blessings in disguise, since

> "God moves in a mysterious way
> His wonders to perform,
> He plants his footsteps in the sea
> And rides upon the storm;"

but there are obvious sunshiny, beautiful and glad experiences in our days which we cannot but enumerate if, with fair and candid minds, we look at their tenor and think of the good hand of our God.

First, there are the blessings which accompany our ordinary health. For many reasons the average rate of health in most communities is higher than it formerly was. People understand that there are hygienic laws to be followed; that sleep, and food, and exercise, comfortable clothing and ventilation have their place in keeping men and women well. We often sin against the body, by overwork or by over indulgence, and nature makes her reprisals, but if we treat the body with the right degree of respect and with common sense we may usually be free from illness. Health means ability to do our work, it means an even disposition, it means nerves sheathed against pain and weariness; it implies strength in reserve, so that we do not always draw upon our balance but have something left over for an emergency. Surely among our chief mercies we should include health, with its attendant grace of serenity, its capacity for enjoyment and its basis for enthusiasm.

Among everyday blessings we may next mention our homes. What joy to turn one's own latch-key at night. What pleasure in laying the tired head on one's own pillow. I never see the crowds of toilers going home after a hard day's work without a pleasant thought of the many little household fires, the children's tumultuous rush to meet their father, the mother's sweet face smiling in the background. "Be it ever so humble there's no place like home." It may be two rooms, it may be a log cabin, it may be a sumptuous mansion; the accident of broad acres or a tiny back yard, of splendor or of poverty, does not affect the home. That is made by the dwellers under the roof; by the love, the gentleness, the sweet converse, the common aims and interests of the family. Bless God for home and a loving greeting may well be our constant prayer.

In every city there are a great multitude of homeless persons, not tramps, nor beggars, but young men who pay for board and lodging, spinsters who have no one closely belonging to them, units who stand alone, solitary who are not in families. The church, the Sunday school, in the great Methodist household of faith the Epworth League, in other denominations the Christian Endeavor Society, or perhaps some beneficent brotherhood or guild, tries to give these lonely ones the substitute for home. The Young Men's and Young Women's Christian Associations wisely and bravely do what they can. But every single Christian home should at times open its doors to the unhomed, asking them to the fireside and the board, bringing them into the charmed circle, and thus arming them against temptation, and providing them with a share in the home's blessings.

Another mercy is opportunity. Be it of what order it may it is one of God's greatest gifts. None are without it. Some have it offered in larger measure than others. Whatever the opportunity may be it is God's open door for you into which you may enter; so count it among your blessings.

Still another source of joy in life comes to us in our children, in our watching their development, in our hope for their future. And our kindred beyond the immediate household, our friends, our neighbors—we cannot omit them from any enumeration of our blessings.

Perhaps we do not often stop to count our church privileges as among our closest joys and our greatest occasions for gratitude. Back of our place in the world's arena is the closet into which we retreat for strength, and our closet is our Holy of Holies; but there is the little prayer-circle, and the larger prayer-meeting, and the assembly of God's people, and the word spoken by the preacher—all as the wind in the sails that sends the vessel onward. There are the summer

gatherings of the saints yearning for a deeper
spiritual life; there are the meetings in the winter when we pray unitedly for revival, and lo!
from the heart of heaven comes the kindling
flame and our souls are burned free from their
worldly dross and seven times refined. In sad
case is that Christian disciple, in woeful case
that Christian congregation, that has no desire
to be revived and seeks not the fanning and the
winnowing of the Holy Ghost.

To leave out of our list of blessings the daily
strife with untoward events, the daily pressure
of the uncongenial, would be to doubt God's wisdom and goodness. "Who art thou," says Car-
lyle, "that complainest of thy life of toil? Complain not. Complain not. Look up, my wearied
brother, see thy fellow Workmen there, in God's
Eternity; surviving there, they alone surviving:
sacred Band of the Immortals, celestial Body-
guard of the Empire of Mankind. . . . To
thee, Heaven, though severe, is not unkind.
Heaven is kind—as a noble mother; as that
Spartan mother, saying, while she gave her son
his shield, 'With it, my son, or upon it!' Thou
too shalt return *home* in honor—to thy far-
distant home in honor; doubt it not—if in the

battle thou keep thy shield. . . . Complain not!"

This strikes a high note. A higher yet they strike who not only refrain from complaint but accept with thankfulness and glad acquiescence in the blessed will of God every single incident, every single companion, every single experience which God sends on the journey; counting each in its degree a blessing.

Says Faber, and we can never quote him too often:

"My heart swells within me in thankfulest joy
  For the faith which to me thou hast given;
For in all thine amazing abundance of gifts
  Thou hast no better gift short of heaven.

"There was darkness in Egypt while Israel had sun,
  And the songs in the cornfields of Goshen were gay;
And the chosen that dwelt 'mid the heathen moved on
  Each threading the gloom with his own private day.

"Ah! so is it now with the church of thy choice;
  Her lands lie in light which to worldlings seems dim;
And each child of that church who must live in dark realms
  Has a sun o'er his head which is only for him."

Among our daily blessings should we not dwell lovingly upon every little bit of work which we are permitted to do for our Lord? On this busy Monday, when the housewife has her somewhat unusual burdens, she may drop a word to the maid in the kitchen which may brighten the day for the maid. The lady going about her shopping may invite the saleswoman behind the counter to attend a gospel meeting in the evening; may promise to be there herself with a sisterly welcome. To each of us, not alone to the ministers ordained and set apart, but to each of us who has joined the company of the Master is a ministry of grace appointed; and it is our crown of rejoicing that we may find the place for it wherever we go. It may be at home, it may be on a journey, it may be on the steamer crossing the ocean, it may be in the conveyance, car or boat, which takes one from house to office, it may be on the farm—wherever you are, and Christ is, and there is a third person yet to be brought to Christ—there is a blessed opportunity for service.

Best and dearest blessing of all is ours when we can comprehend even a little of the great love of our Lord, and for a little time lose ourselves in adoration of him.

> "When Jesus went from Bethany
>   Joy bloomed before him like the May.
> The beauty and the mystery
>   Of something heavenly brimmed the day."

When Jesus comes to any earthly home the light as of the Father's face enters there and abides. When Jesus goes forth the light remains, for the beloved goes forth too, and walks with the Master all the day long, and at night the Master returns and sups with his disciple. Who shall measure such divine blessedness?

CHAPTER XXVIII

Looking unto Jesus

There are many roads to the house of good
cheer—roads of congenial associations, of pleasant employments, of joy in attainments, and of
happy endeavors. But the road which is
straightest and surest is the road at the entrance
of which is inscribed "Looking unto Jesus."
They who look unto their Lord as the flower
turns to the sun cannot lose the way to ease of
mind and hope of heart, to cheerful to-days and
trustful to-morrows. Safe with Jesus is their
past, serene in Jesus is their present, secure in
Jesus is their future. Forever, thus looking
and waiting, they renew their strength. They
may be old, they may be suffering, they may be
in prison, they may be nigh unto death, but
conditions matter not; the disciples, looking
unto Jesus, see his face smiling on them and
nothing can detract from their courage.

"Jesus, my Love, my chief delight,
For thee I long, for thee I pray,
Amid the shadows of the night,
Amid the burdens of the day."

Rapt in the ecstasy of adoration, what trial or trouble can weigh the Christian down? Do we look unto Jesus in worship, as we ought? Is our earliest waking thought of his goodness and his beauty? Do we dwell on his grace, remembering him as the chiefest among ten thousand and altogether lovely? It was said of Robert McCheyne, of Dundee, Scotland, that he so communed with Jesus that his prayers and his sermons dripped with the perfume of his love, and that he so enjoyed that love-letter of the Old Testament, the Song of Solomon, that he had found texts for discourses in its every chapter.

Ah, friends, our heart's longing, our heart's cry should be for Jesus, so that our looking unto him might be always in worshipful adoration.

> "My soul amid this stormy world
> Is like some fluttered dove,
> And fain would be as swift of wing
> To flee to him I love."

Our looking unto Jesus too must be that we may receive his orders and be quick to obey them. To one who saw him through the rifted skies, one arrested on his way to commit a great crime against the saints, Christ revealed himself in a glimpse of fire, and from that moment

Paul's looking was merged in an earnest, reverent petition: "Lord, what wilt thou have me to do?" We know how delightful is the home life where each wills to do the other's will, and God's will is triumphant over all. Any life which looks up constantly to Christ, in entire submission and joyful desire to hear and obey, must be full of cheer, and equally so must any home thus keyed to perfect harmony be a place of blessedness.

We need to examine ourselves to discover whether we are making any reservation in our yielding to the will of the Master. We are sometimes reluctant to engage in a plain duty because our taking part in it will render us conspicuous, or lest we shall be charged with inconsistency by those whom we meet. Looking unto Jesus, there should be no withholding of anything we have, no withdrawal of anything we are, when our Captain bids us advance; there should be no regretting thought or fretfulness when he tells us to stay where we are and be for a time inactive. There are those whom he seems to lay for a while on the shelf; if this be his will, we must find our joy and our reward in thus awaiting his pleasure.

We may look unto Jesus from the desk, from the army post, from the tent, from the anvil. Surely our looking should be so evident that those around us will recognize us for children of the King. "I sat by a man for ten years," said one, "we did our work side by side, but I never dreamed that he was a Christian." The man may have had a similar absence of impression concerning the speaker.

In politics men are not slow to show the side they take. Why should they be less awake to the need of showing their colors when their relation to Christ is involved; in speech or in silence, shall not the truly earnest and sincere man find out a way to show where he stands?

Looking unto Jesus will keep us from being difficult to live with. Good people not a few are over sensitive, are easily hurt, are irritable about trifles. The remedy for the fretfulness which so often degenerates into morbidness is found in continual looking unto Jesus.

In a partnership of complete affection the subconscious habit is one of resting upon and referring to the ceaseless love which each heart feels sure of; it is not with effort or with study that husband turns to wife or wife to husband

in the sweet intercourse of daily life and love.
There is no jarring note, the melody is unbroken.

Our Lord himself has compared to marriage,
the closest of earthly friendships, the bond
which unites his church to him. The looking
unto him of the Christian may become automatic, like breathing; it may never be interrupted; it may lift every day and hour into a
mystic loveliness, such as floods the sunset sky
when the gold and amber and opal of the Western horizon surpass in splendor the colors ever
seen on any palette under the heavens themselves.

"Who shall separate us from the love of
Christ?" They who know its inner sweetness,
its strength, and its amazing tenderness, know
that, whatever else breaks, that cable will hold
forever.

> "O Jesus, Jesus, dearest Lord,
>   Forgive me if I say,
> For very love, thy sacred name
>   A thousand times a day.
>
> "For thou to me art all in all,
>   My honor and my wealth,
> My heart's desire, my body's strength,
>   My soul's eternal health.

"Burn, burn, O Love! within my heart,
  Burn fiercely night and day,
Till all the dross of earthly loves
  Is burned and burned away.

"O Jesus! Jesus! sweetest Lord,
  What art Thou not to me?
Each hour brings joy before unknown;
  Each day new liberty."

CHAPTER XXIX

THE SUNNY HEART

WE have many gray days in our winters, but on the whole the days of clearest sunshine far outnumber them. I heard a dear woman thank God the other day for having sent a bright afternoon for a meeting, and I thought how right that was, and how often we omitted to praise him for good weather. With the shepherd of Salisbury Plain, we ought to be grateful for whatever weather comes, and when we reach that point of acquiescent praise we shall have sunny skies in the soul.

"Do you find it possible," said my friend Eleanora, "to be anything but perfunctory in your keeping of Thanksgiving? What does it amount to in your life?" This was just before a Thanksgiving Day.

"I hope, dear," I answered, "that I am making every day a day of giving thanks. I am sometimes overwhelmed when I begin to count up my mercies; they are so many, for the bright days so far exceed the dark ones, that I cannot help having a song in my heart all the time. But when Thanksgiving Day returns it always brings its own proper observance with it—that is, if one is patriotic; and, too, if one believes in God."

Eleanora mused awhile. "I'm not sure that I am patriotic," she said. "I want those poor men of ours to come home safely from the Philippines, and I want peace to prevail on land and sea, and I don't wish to see the rich so very rich nor the poor so very poor, and I'm sure that saloons are rampageous, and that the Sabbath is profaned, and—for me—the times are out of joint. No, I am not really thankful."

"I suppose we may all find points to criticise in the management of public affairs, and features in our social economy to regret; but we have not the responsibility of ordering nor of carrying on the routine of this great nation, and therefore it is not worth while for us to be pessimistic or fault-finding. And just at this moment people are striving earnestly to put down intemperance, and, as never before, business is making a strong fight against it. A drinking man cannot hold a place on a railroad, nor in a factory, nor anywhere in which his habit of life can endanger other people's lives or menace valuable property. This one fact, if there were no other, is a mighty weapon of attack upon the saloon.

"The remedy for our violation of the Sabbath will be found in a deepening of the spiritual life of individuals and in a quickening of the personal conscience. There is at the moment a wide spreading effort for revival, and all over our country, in groups and prayer circles and meetings, Christians are seeking the presence and power of the Lord. Once the Holy Spirit descends again in the church there will be a toning up of public sentiment on the Sabbath question and the world will respect the wish and follow the lead of God's people about observing God's day. I think we should thank God especially, this year, for the signs of promise in the sky."

This was a very long speech, and Eleanora rose when I had finished it, took her leave and went away. I was doubtful whether my monologue had done her any good. It at least set me to thinking quite seriously, and I began to go over in my own mind certain reasons for being very thankful in this good year of our Lord.

Among positive occasions for gratitude at present our magnificent harvests come easily first. Never has there been a more tremendous yield of wheat and corn to reward the farmer. America may feed the world from her granaries if she choose. Our vineyards have been purple and black and white and ruby and amber with grapes which have been refreshing to the palate and beautiful to the eye. The vines have been weighted with the luscious store, the clusters have been exquisite. Nature has surpassed herself, and in lavish bounty has spread every board. Think of her oats, her rye, her pears, her cherries, her plums. And as for apples, in their choice varieties, in their fragrant ripeness, in their splendid colorings and multitudinous array the year has been one of exceeding wealth. Seek-no-furthers, Baldwins, pippins, greenings—their names are on the orchard catalogue and their golden or ruby globes are in our bins and cellars. What would the housekeeper do without apples? What would the country boy do if he had no apples for his school luncheon or his evening feast? Pies, and preserves and jellies, and many a toothsome puff and pudding owe their sweetness to the apple, and 1899 wears as one of its peculiar jewels the glory of being an apple year. For fruit of the tree, of the bush, and the vine, let us give thanks.

Looking over the last twelve months accidents and horrors and calamities have been comparatively few, and dreadful crimes have been less frequent than usual. Also labor and capital seem better to have understood one another and the friction between them has been minimized. Taking it all in all, we have passed through a year of great internal tranquillity, of much general prosperity, and of notably good times. Shall we not therefore thank God and take courage? The Lord who has brought us thus far on our way will surely carry us through.

When we come to the reckoning of personal reasons for thanksgiving every heart and every home must keep tally of its own delights. For health and strength, for the dear one's convalescence, for the pleasant outing, for the happy times among ourselves, for the new baby, for the lengthened life of honored old people, for the success of the son at college or in business, for our ships that have come safe home from long and perilous voyages on the tempestuous sea, for our neighbors and friends, we must praise and thank the good Lord.

For any new sight of the Master's face vouchsafed to us in the retirement of the closet, for help and stimulus which have come to us when we have read our Bible or heard a sermon, for any song in the night, we should not fail to render our thanks. In a world full of unknown possibilities, we are like children rocked in the cradle and crooned over by the mother, so good is our Lord to us every hour.

We may have some negative reasons for thanksgiving too; in that things have been no worse: always a legitimate cause for praise. That we have had no Dreyfus case to shame us in this nation must be enumerated among our reasons for grateful memory. We who have small boys may be glad that they are not oftener brought home to us maimed from the football field, and thankful that most of their wounds are so soon and so easily healed.

In all seriousness, friends, should we not take pains to cultivate a continual habit of thankfulness? This would help to make us optimistic; we should not go about with long faces nor look too much on the dark side. The good hand of our God is upon us, saving us from dangers seen and unseen; let us therefore take the cup of thanksgiving and call upon his name.

Our prayers are too often narrowed down to a mere asking for what we want, a mere petitioning for favors at the throne. The soul rises into a purer ether and knows a dearer joy when prayer is largely composed of gratitude, when we are lifted up in contemplation to heights of a divine and restful calm.

A good exercise for you and for me just now might be with pencil and paper to set down, in orderly sequence, where we can plainly see them, our private reasons for being thankful to an overruling Providence. Then when Thanksgiving Day dawns let us go to church in the good old way to acknowledge national blessings, mercies to the commonwealth.

Our dinner table will be happiest if we gather about it the whole clan, our kith and kin, from the silver-haired grandsire to the baby in the high chair, and the viands will taste the sweeter if we have sent a portion to the widow around the corner, to the ragged little newsboy, to the out-at-elbows tramp tempted for once by fire and food to enter a beneficent mission. Do not let us forget the college settlement, nor the industrial homes, the orphanage, nor any other charity on Thanksgiving Day. Even the prisoner behind the barred gates and stone walls should on this day have a gleam of friendly sympathy and loving charity thrown across his hard and bitter pathway.

If possible, let the home gathering be very complete when the Thanksgiving gala day returns. This is an American custom which should not fall into desuetude.

Good Dr. Cuyler, writing of Christian experience, exclaims:

"In the depths of a devout, loyal, praying and trustful heart Christ kindles a glow that cannot be drowned by pains of sickness, or storms of adversity, or even by the tears of bereavement. One of the most sunny Christians I ever knew was racked with the tortures of a rheumatism that had distorted every limb. In the darkest hours Jesus can give triumphant 'songs in the night.' When Dr. Horace Bushnell was writing a letter of consolation to a brother who had met with a severe bereavement he said, 'Soften your grief by *much thanksgiving.*' Gratitude for what Jesus has done for us sinners, for what he gives us every day, for what he has laid up in store for us in heaven, and for the solid assurance that we shall meet our loved ones there—such gratitude can pour its rays into our hearts and put a new song into our mouths.

"Is it possible for all of us who claim to be Christ's followers to live steadily in the bright sunshine of Christ's love? It must be possible; for the Master never bids us do what we cannot perform or be what we cannot become. Sinless perfection may not be attainable in this world, or unalloyed happiness. But there is one thing which all of Christ's redeemed people can do, and that is to keep themselves in the atmosphere of his love. 'Abide ye in my love.' It is our fault and our shame that we spend so many days in the chilling fogs or under the heavy clouds of unbelief, or in the bleak atmosphere of conformity to the world."

Tauler wrote tersely, by way of admonition:

"Think not that God will always be caressing his children, or shine upon their head, or kindle their hearts, as he does at the first. He does so only to lure us to himself, as the falconer lures the falcon with its gay hood. Our Lord works with his children so as to teach them afterwards to work themselves; as he bade Moses to make the tables of stone after the pattern of the first, which he had made himself. Thus, after a time, God allows man to depend upon himself, and no longer enlightens, and stimulates, and rouses him. We must stir up and rouse ourselves, and be content to leave off learning, and no more enjoy feeling and fire, and must now serve the Lord with strenuous industry and at our own cost. Our Lord acts as a prudent father, who, while his children are young, lets them live at his cost, and manages everything for them. What is needful for them he provides, and lets them go and play; and so long as this lasts they are at leisure, free from care, happy, and generous at their father's expense. Afterwards he gives a portion of his estate into their own hands, because he will have them to take care of themselves and earn their own living, to leave off childish play, and thus learn how to grow rich."

We may at least refrain from ever expressing dissatisfaction with God's dealings and discontent with our circumstances. By the time to-morrow reaches us to-day's discomfort will have fled. Each day bears only its own burden, and every burden is bound together and labeled, "By the will of God." Are we depending **for** our joy, not on our earthly environment, but on that which hour by hour the Lord bestows? Then shall we ever despond? Shall we not always wear the brightness of heaven on our faces and in our hearts? Let us constantly pray:

> "Drop Thy sweet dews of quietness
>   Till all our strivings cease;
> Take from our souls the strain and stress
> And let our ordered lives confess
>   The beauty of Thy peace."

CHAPTER XXX

Beyond the Horizon's Rim

One of these days it will all be over,
  Sorrow and laughter, loss and gain,
Meetings and partings of friend and lover,
  Joy that was often tinged with pain.
One of these days will our hands be folded,
  One of these days will the work be done,
Finished the pattern our lives have molded,
  Ended our labor beneath the sun.

One of these days will the heartache leave us,
  One of these days will the burden drop;
Never again shall a hope deceive us,
  Never again shall our progress stop.
Freed from the blight of the vain endeavor,
  Winged with the health of immortal life,
One of these days we shall quit forever
  All that is vexing in earthly strife.

One of these days we shall know the reason,
  Haply, of much that perplexes now;
One of these days, in the Lord's good season,
  Light of his peace shall adorn the brow.
Blessèd, though out of tribulation,
  Lifted to dwell in his sun-bright smile,
Happy to share the great salvation,
  Can we not patiently tarry awhile?

The eye which gazes beyond the horizon's
rim and expects the hour when the day shall

break in the new life above may grow weary,
but it will not grow discouraged. For we walk
by the starlight of the promises as well as by the
sunshine of daily mercies. We need never fear.
One who knows our infirmities is always at our
side.

The pleasure of good company is with us, too,
on the road home. True, there remaineth much
land to be possessed. Millions of our fellow
beings are yet in the darkness of heathenism.

The false gods are not yet overthrown nor are
the idols utterly abolished. But we may help
send the Gospel, and we shall gain a blessing if
we do so in the spirit of the little East-end
London girl who wanted to do her share:

> It was only a silver sixpence,
>   Battered and worn and old,
> But worth to the child that held it
>   As much as a piece of gold.
>
> A poor little crossing-sweeper,
>   In the wind and rain all day—
> For one who gave her a penny
>   There were twenty who bade her nay.
>
> But she carried the bit of silver—
>   A light in her steady face,
> And her step on the crowded pavement
>   Full of a childish grace—

Straight to the tender pastor;
  And "Send it," she said, "for me,
Dear sir, to the heathen children
  On the other side of the sea.

"Let it help in telling the story
  Of the love of the Lord most high,
Who came from the world of glory
  For a sinful world to die."

"Send only half of it, Maggie,"
  The good old minister said,
"And keep the rest for yourself, dear;
  You need it for daily bread."

"Ah, sir," was the ready answer,
  In the blessed Bible words,
"I would rather lend it to Jesus:
  For the silver and gold are the Lord's,

"And the copper will do for Maggie."
  I think, if we all felt so,
The wonderful message of pardon
  Would soon through the dark earth go.

Soon should the distant mountains
  And the far-off isles of the sea
Hear of the great salvation
  And the truth that makes men free.

Alas! do we not too often
  Keep our silver and gold in store,
And grudgingly part with our copper,
  Counting the pennies o'er,

And claiming in vain the blessing,
  That the Master gave to one
Who dropped her mites as the treasure
  A whole day's toil had won?

A toil-worn returned missionary was addressing a group of women the other day, and she
said, with the sound of tears in her voice, "Oh,
you would love to help the Lord's work on if
you *knew* about it." The trouble too often is,
friends, that we do not know. We look at our
own garden gate, not at the rim of the sky
where disappears the ship which bears along the
foreign missionaries going on their errands of
love. Not all of us are to blame for this indifference. Our city households do, some of them
at least, keep in touch with Ceylon, India,
China, and our workers there. Very frequently
one discovers in country homes, remote from
the railroad, a great deal of good periodical
literature. Especially are some of these households well informed as to foreign and home
missions. Inquiring of a busy house mistress,
whose home had been filled with summer
boarders from June until September, when she
found time to read all her books and magazines,
the answer came promptly, "I read up in the
long winter evenings. My family is small then,
and I have plenty of time; I just save everything till then, and I go through my pile from
first to last." Certainly there is no lack either

of interest or of information in and about the Lord's work on the part of these busy, hard-working, but most intelligent women.

It is by reading and by attending meetings of prayer for missions that we get to know about and to love them and their various phases of effort. There are the preaching, the visiting, the teaching, the translating, the comforting ministrations to mind and body, which compose the several sorts of work at a mission station. Are we praying for all, aiding all, giving to all? Some days are brighter to us than others because we may say at nightfall,

God gave me something very sweet to be mine own
    this day—
A precious opportunity a word for Christ to say;
A soul that my desire might reach; a work to do for
    him;
And now I thank him for this grace, ere yet the light
    grows dim.

No service that he sends me on can be so welcome aye:
To guide a pilgrim's weary feet within the narrow
    way;
To share the loving Shepherd's quest, and so, by brake
    and fen,
To find for him his wandering lambs, the erring sons
    of men.

I did not seek this blessed thing; it came a rare sur-
    prise,
Flooding my heart with dearest joy, as, lifting wistful
    eyes,

Heaven's light upon a dear one's face shone plain and
    clear on mine:
And there an unseen third, I felt, was waiting—One
    divine.

So in this twilight hour I kneel, and pour my grateful
    thought
In song and prayer to Jesus for the gifts this day hath
    brought.
Sure never service is so sweet, nor life hath so much
    zest,
As when he bids me speak for him, and then he does
    the rest.

I may be mistaken, but as I have gone about
the world it has seemed to me that the happiest
and most gracious family life has existed where
the family looked ever beyond the horizon's rim,
and lived as united by a common bond in Christ.
We cannot but be sweet and gentle if we are imi-
tators of him who "pleased not himself." We
cannot but be happy if we have a common aim,
a common interest, higher than mere worldli-
ness and money making, and the habit of constant reference of every little and large thing to
the Lord as the arbiter of our lives; yet, gazing
heavenward, we are for the present held fast by
cords of might to the earth wherein we dwell,
and it is worth our while to consider our ways
in the household.

Our manners in the family are very apt to be the sincere expressions, as they are the unconscious revelations, of our prevailing and dominant states of mind. Character is indicated by the tricks of speech and of gesture, the tones of voice, the politeness or the rudeness of daily deportment, and by a hundred small things which are automatic; things of which we take no note, perhaps of which we are quite unaware. Just as an habitually gentle and controlled person has a quiet and serene face, and as a tempestuous and unrestrained nature writes its record on the countenance, so the manners of a family set it apart as well bred or the reverse, and the family air stamps each individual of the clan.

Why do people residing under the same roof gain a certain resemblance? Originally, it may be, their features were cast in different molds; they started in being unlike, but time, and familiarity, and an incessant process of unconscious imitation, has brought about a marked similarity, so that the loving husband and wife actually look alike, with a subtler and more spiritual likeness than the mere surface resemblance of kinship.

When the overwrought and overtired mother scolds her fractious child, allowing her fretfulness to sharpen her accents and speaking with the stormy emphasis of anger, she does not mean permanently to influence her little one's manner, but she is doing so nevertheless. The child grows querulous, reflecting the nervous susceptibility to strain which makes the mother unamiable. Placidity, serenity, a tranquil calm of strength and sweetness in combination, seem to have vanished from many homes wherein people are hurried and worried, distraught and care-laden.

Our manners may help to control our minds. So subtle is the connection between body and spirit, whenever we can absolutely require of the former perfect repose, the repression of impatient movements and of irritated speech, the spirit gains time to conquer itself and finds its lost poise. To go alone, sit perfectly still and refuse to allow even so much as a frown or a pucker upon one's face, to do this when circumstances are peculiarly trying or when one is aware that weariness will presently degenerate to crossness, may save one from a humiliating outbreak, and add permanently to the stock of self-control which we all need as capital for life.

Family manners, apart from the relations of parents and children, which imply a reciprocal consideration, are apt to suffer from too much candor. We speak with great plainness in the circle of our own kindred; we comment too freely on foibles; we express the contrary opinion too readily and with too little courtesy. A slight infusion of formality never harms social intercourse, either in the family or elsewhere.

Beyond this too common mistake of an over-bluntness and brusque freedom in the manners of a household, in some of our homes there is a greater fault even—a lack of demonstration. There is the deepest, sincerest love in the home, the brothers and sisters would cheerfully die for one another if so great a sacrifice were demanded, but the love is ice-locked behind a barrier of reserve. Caresses are infrequent, words of affection are seldom spoken. It may be urged with truth and some show of reason that in the very homes where this absence of demonstration is most marked there is complete mutual understanding, and no possibility of doubt or misgiving, and, so far as it goes, this is well. But often young hearts long unspeakably for some gentle sign of love's presence—the lingering touch of a tender hand on the head, the good-night kiss, the word of praise, the recognition of affection. Older hearts, too, are sometimes empty, and many of us, younger and older, are kept on short rations all our lives, when our right, on our Father's road to our Father's house, is to be fed with the finest of the wheat, and enough of it; just as those who ate manna in the wilderness had always an entire provision, not a stinted supply.

Another suggestion which should not be overlooked is the importance of politeness to the little ones. To snub a small laddie needlessly, to order a child about on errands here and there instead of civilly preferring a request as one does to an older person, in each case is an invasion of the rights of childhood. The child to whom everybody practices politeness will in turn be himself ready to oblige and agreeable in manner, for the stamp of the family is as plainly to be seen on us every one as the stamp of the mint on the coin, and it is as indelible for time—and why not, also, for eternity?

A child sometimes slips away from our grasp

all in a moment. The sweet young daughter of
the house was going to school, week before last.
Yesterday, after a very brief illness, she was
not, for God had taken her. The baby went to
bed well, but croup came in the night and a
mother's arms are empty. Oh, the deep grief
over tiny graves, the scalding tears that blind us
when we look at vacant chairs! While they are
with us let us do all we can to make our dar-
lings happy; while they remain let our tones be
sweet, our acts unselfish, our love unstinted.
When God calls them let us have no remorse
which might have been avoided, but let us not
refuse consolation, for,

They never quite leave us, our friends who have passed
Through the shadow of death to the sunlight above;
A thousand sweet memories are holding them fast
To the places they bless with their presence and love.

The work which they left and the books which they
    read
Speak mutely, though still with an eloquence rare;
And the songs that they sung, and dear words they
    said,
Yet linger and sigh on the desolate air.

And oft when alone, and as oft in the throng,
Or when evil allures us or sin draweth nigh,
A whisper comes gently, "Nay, do not the wrong,"
And we feel that our weakness is pitied on high.

Trustful To-morrows

In the dew-threaded morn and the opaline eve,
When the children are merry or crimsoned with sleep,
We are comforted, even as lonely we grieve,
For the thoughts of their rapture forbids us to weep.

We toil at our tasks in the burden and heat
Of life's passionate noon : they are folded in peace.
It is well.   We rejoice that their heaven is sweet,
And one day for us will all bitterness cease.

We, too, will go home o'er the river of rest,
As the strong and the lovely before us have gone ;
Our sun will go down in the beautiful west
To rise in the glory that circles the throne.

Until then we are bound by our love and our faith
To the saints who are walking in Paradise fair.
They have passed beyond sight, at the touching of
       death,
But they live, like ourselves, in God's infinite care.

Warning

In the time of our fullness and thrift,
   Ere the time of our loss and our dole,
Let the angels who guard us uplift
   A warning to every soul.
Oh ! heed it and hear it, lest all unaware
We waken some day to the gloom of despair.

We shall never be sorry for love ;
   For the words that are patient and sweet ;
For the hardness repressed,
For the anger unguessed,
   For the grace that is swift to entreat.

We shall never be sorry for hope
  That heartened the weak and the tried,
That made them the bolder to cope
  With the evil one, close to their side;
For the pity we've shown
To the souls that alone
  Were stemming some fierce, rushing tide.

We shall never be sorry for care
  To the old or the little ones given;
Nor ever regret the swift prayer
  That went to our Father in heaven
For meekness and cheer
When the outlook was drear,
  For faith when our courage was riven.

In the time of our fullness and thrift,
  Ere the time of our dole and our loss,
Let the angels who guard us uplift
  A voice against cleaving to dross;
Let us hear it and heed it, lest all unaware
We waken some day to the gloom of despair.

CHAPTER XXXI

The Habit of Holding On

Among excellent wearing habits, in this age of haste and competition, we should set a high value on that of holding on. Having decided on a course of action, looked at it from every point of view, and taken stock of ourselves and of the situation, we should first kneel down alone in our closets, or with our families if the matter concern them, and ask God's blessing. Let the errand be what it may, the disciple does not go forward without the Master's assurance that he is with him. Next, we should begin with earnestness, zeal, and discretion; enthusiasm held in check by wisdom and knowledge. Last, we should hold on.

The world highly values success, especially the success which is apparent. In no walk of life is success attainable by the man or the woman who has not acquired persistence, the art of holding on. In the inspired page of Revelation the promise is, over and over, made of reward to "him that overcometh." Overcoming is holding on.

We see children full of the zest of beginning. The first chapter of the new book, the first week at the new school, the opening tasks of the new term, fill them with eager delight. It is the *élan* of the novel enterprise which excites and stimulates them to effort. So in Leagues, and Endeavor societies of every variety, there is apt to be great ardor at the outset. The testing time arrives when the year has reached its middle period, when the attraction of novelty has waned, when what is needed is not an enthusiastic start, but steady staying power. Blessings on those young people who have the good habit of holding on; who do not dread the quiet performance of obscure duties; who can march on even when the music in advance is temporarily silent.

Our greatest sailors and soldiers, our most eminent statesmen, our most renowned missionaries, our scholars famed for research and accuracy, have had the habit of holding on.

You are perhaps very near the foot of the ladder to-day, and to climb high will mean a struggle full of pluck and of dogged determination. Remember that God has given you a foothold, and that he now expects you valiantly to fight for yourself. Lose no advantage, never shirk a hard task, be courteous, be obliging, be unselfish; but through every opposition, and even in the face of disaster and disappointment, hold on in your way.

It is a fine thing to make defeat your stepping stone to victory.

There are failures which God sends and God plans, and which are in his sight far more radiant than any human success. There are those carried wounded to the rear, or dropped out of the procession, whom God honors with his "Well done, good and faithful servant!" But of these it may be said without hesitation that they possessed the habit of holding on to what seemed to them right; that they did their duty manfully, and rounded out their day's work, more anxious about the work than about the wages.

I would warn those who would enjoy cheerful to-days and inherit trustful to-morrows against being over solicitous for the success which is estimated in money. Ours is a commercial age, and we are apt, because it is in the air about us, to admire too highly the acquisition of wealth. As a means to an end, and that end the service of God and the elevation of man, wealth is desirable. For all else, the words of the wise man remain eternally judicious, "Give me neither poverty nor riches." The middle course is the happy course. Work done for mercenary reasons alone is never the highest and the best work. "Give us the glory of going on," sings the poet.

To hold on as the scientific student does in the laboratory, that he may gain knowledge along lines which will alleviate suffering and mitigate disease, to hold on as the general does when the campaign is a long one and the odds are against him, to hold on as the mother does through the years when her little ones are in the crib and the nursery, to hold on as the pastor does in his quiet round of loving ministry, studying, toiling, striving, comforting—thus to hold on is to win and keep the divine favor.

Thus holding on, we may

> "Look up and not down;
> Look forward and not back;
> Look out and not in; and
> Lend a hand."

Away back in the second book of Chronicles we are told of the good King Hezekiah, that "he wrought that which was good and right and faithful before the Lord his God. And in every work that he began in the service of the house of God, and in the law, and in the commandments, to seek his God, he did it with all his heart, and prospered."

King Hezekiah had mastered the art of holding on.

CHAPTER XXXII

ONE WORD MORE FOR OUR GIRLS

To many a girl the abandonment of her hope to attend college is the greatest disappointment of her young life. Her mother needs her at home, or her father thinks she has had a sufficient amount of school discipline, or there is not money enough to make a college education practicable—for some reason or other the step cannot be taken; and the young woman is obliged to make her plans along different lines from those which she had intended. In the case of one exceptionally gifted girl, very dear to me in later years, her mother's death throwing upon the brave young shoulders the care and oversight of a family of small brothers and sisters made college impossible. She could not be spared from the desolate home, where she speedily became the sister-mother and the homemaker and housekeeper.

Another young woman, prepared for college and anxious to go because of a genuine enthusiasm for learning, was compelled at twenty years of age to resign her ambition lest she should use means which were required for the education of younger children. Twelve years later this woman, who had bided her time, never complaining, never querulous, invariably patient, cheerful and bright, was enabled to fulfill her desire and she is in college now; resolutely taking up the old tools and studying happily among her juniors, with whom she is a great favorite. And no wonder: at heart she is as young as the youngest.

I have found it my greatest comfort, girls, in every situation to say to myself, "This is God's appointment for me, and it therefore must be right." When we accept God's will as best it is a pillow under the head than which nothing could be softer and more peaceful. If it is for our advantage to go or to stay we do not know, but God knows; and all our days are arranged for us according to his plan.

Supposing, therefore, that college is out of the question, what hinders a bright, keen-witted girl from making the very best of her time and talents at home? She may take up a Chautauqua course, or a course prescribed by the Epworth League, and her reading may be definite and systematic, not haphazard and occasional. She will see for herself that while the newspaper keeps one informed as to current events, and well-selected fiction pleases the imagination, yet neither the newspaper nor the novel can alone give a woman a cultivated mind or discipline her intellect. If she is wise, and in earnest, she will set herself to a resolute and persistent and thorough study of some branch of science or some period of history. One girl found it feasible to follow her brother's college course at home, and she took up in her own room, and without the spur of emulation or the assistance of a tutor, everything that he did—Latin, Greek, French, philosophy and mathematics—slighting nothing, and keeping pace with him to the end; the only difference then being that he had a diploma and she had none. All the substantial good of college training belonged to her as well as to him.

Many girls have not the leisure for so much consecutive work as was here gone over. Do not despair on that account. A half hour devoted to study every day, without a break, will give results at the end of the year which will be simply surprising. I have seen a young woman occupied in a factory in New York, toiling early and late and having no place at home to study, who, availing herself of the reading room of a working girl's club, has made herself familiar with English history from the earliest days until the Victorian era. Everything against her, but courage and will and a love of books carrying her splendidly forward!

Avail yourself of the lecture courses open to you, near your home, and ask your friends who have gone farther than yourself for a little enlightenment when you reach a difficult place. Libraries and books of reference may be found in most towns; if you have none in your neighborhood your pastor will probably be willing to lend you books or to guide you in their purchase. Little by little add to your stock of literature, buying only after careful thought as to whether you are sure you need the book on which your desire has been fixed. A dictionary and an encyclopedia are immeasurably valuable to a student who is not near a library.

By the daily practice of reading good books, and by seeking the friendship of refined and intelligent men and women, you will gain an appreciation of literature and of scholarship quite equal to that which your friend obtains in her life of the school. Do not suffer yourself to be slipshod and careless as to your vocabulary, to use slang, or to drop into provincialisms. It is true that very well informed persons do use these, but they do not belong to a lady, and they are blots on her manner of expression—tattered fringe on an elegant garment. Better be precise and pedantic than heedless of your mother-tongue and ungrammatical in conversation or writing. Remember that there is nothing open to us so educational and so improving on its very lowest plane as regular attendance at a place of worship. Merely always going to church and giving one's attention fully to the preacher, merely dwelling on the themes he touches, largely helps those who must have culture but cannot have college.

But if one does go, and many of our young women are thus privileged, let her determine to be on the Lord's side from the outset. None of us can stay in utter solitude, without comradeship, and be happy or entirely useful. That idea of life which implies isolation is not wholesome. It is worth while for us to think a little about our friends—what we do for them and what they do for us.

Should an entire class assembled in college for the first time be composed altogether of strangers, some from Kansas, some from Tennessee, some from Florida, others from Maine, still others from Texas, New York, Ohio and Colorado, with a sprinkling of girls from the Sandwich Islands and Japan, it would not be long before the various young women would shake apart from the mass and settle into groups. These groups would again subdivide into smaller circles, and the circles would finally fall into the partnership of individuals. The closer welding of the intimate friendship of the twos would not interfere with the pleasant mingling of the threes and fours and sevens, while over all, and uniting all, would be the beautiful and subtle growth and continuance of the class feeling; a sentiment which survives through life and is one of life's most delightful experiences. The girl from Texas might find congenial qualities and similar tastes in the girl from Maine, and the soft-voiced Kentuckian might choose for her dearest confidante a crisp and clever young woman from New York. Inevitably each would modify the other and help the other on.

This is one of the best offices of friendship— to be helpful where one can. I never thought very highly of the plan that friends should candidly tell each other of their faults. The office of critic is rather ungracious, and very, very few persons are able to listen without annoyance to the recital of their defects, as seen by even friendly eyes. As a matter of course a girl expects reproof or suggestion at times from her mother, or her teacher, but she does not care for it from her school or college friends, and, even if she is equally candid in return, the mutual inspection is usually fatal to affection. Far better it is to help by example; by being so true, so straightforward and so unselfish that your friends emulate you. To live with some people is to be lifted to a broader and higher plane and a purer air. In forming our college friendships we are probably entering into pleasant bonds which will never be unloosed, and we should try to be so sincerely loving that our friends will receive from us only our best. Most of us make unconscious revelations of ourselves when we are off guard. Our living should be of an order so pure and sweet that we would never be afraid of being found out; that we might always be sure that in our most intimate moments nothing in us should hurt another soul.

What do we ask of our dear friends? For one thing, entire trust. Girls use many caressing phrases and tender names to each other, and there are girls whose natures seem to demand a good deal of demonstration. Now, there is no harm in this, to a certain extent, but the love which can go without much verbal expression is apt to be the more deeply rooted. Jealousy should never be permitted to creep into friendship, and a girl should take herself at once to task if she perceives that she is entertaining suspicions of her friend, or is vexed at the coming of a third person into the compact.

We are many-sided beings, and our natures have many needs; a great capacity for loving is a splendid equipment for life. Let us not dwarf and stunt ourselves by selfish narrowness, and above all let us shield our hearts from distrust; from readiness to imagine affronts and from that over-sensitiveness which believes that our friend could intentionally wound us.

To our friends we should give sympathy; should be interested in their endeavors and ambitions, should be ready to listen when they have anything to tell and to counsel if they ask advice. The foundation of sympathy is unselfishness, "a heart at leisure from itself." Simply to be glad with others and sad with others is not enough; we should go farther, and live in our friends' lives. We may not know their people but we should try to care about them, and nothing which even remotely concerns our comrades should seem to us of no moment. Sympathy, trust and common interests will very closely unite those who are thrown together in the contact of daily life through a period of four successive years.

I cannot conceive of an enduring friendship in which there is in both parties no love to Christ. The disciple of Jesus has something so lovely and dear as a part of her life that she longs to share it. Christ is so much more to her than any earthly friend that aversion to him, or indifference, or hostility, if persevered in, must repel her from anyone, however otherwise attractive. Alienation from him must deeply grieve the true disciple. There is no re-

lation so perfect as that of two congenial
natures who love the Master and are trying to
follow him.   Of this I am sure, that the Christ-
lover will never rest until she has brought her
friend to the blessedness which she knows; and
that, if her friend persistently refuses Christ
and turns from him, in the end, and from
the operation of a law as relentless as that of
gravitation, their friendship will cease.   For
friendship demands confidence and sympathy
and a life in common interests day by day, and
these cannot exist in perfection between those
who love Christ and those who hate him.

Never Too Soon

Never too soon? For what, my dear?
  Never too soon to choose the best,
And set the mark of your living clear,
  And bring your soul to the highest test.

Never too soon to stand for God,
  To lift the banner of Christ on high;
The foe with his legions is all abroad,
  And his challenging giants are drawing nigh.

Our girls are interested in deciding on their
future employments and callings.   Among the
newer avocations journalism beckons many, for
the reason, above others, that it may more read-

ily be entered than law or medicine or teaching. The young woman who expects to teach needs very thorough preparation, and, in these days, must if possible specialize. If she wishes to instruct in the higher mathematics, or in art, she will be the better equipped if after receiving her diploma she can secure several years of postgraduate study either at home or abroad. If she is to be a doctor, the medical college exacts a regular and severely rigid course of training, and there is no royal road hewed for the feet of the feminine lawyer. She must read grave legal books, and serve a precisely similar apprenticeship to that demanded by the authorities from her brother.

A young woman must begin as a journalist at the foot of the ladder. She may go into the newspaper arena from the high school. Several of our most successful women editors have never been to college. Her equipment will be, an outfit of good sense, mental alertness, a talent for pleasing others in selection, obedience to orders, and ability to read, to spell, and to write good clear English. Much familiarity with Latin and Greek does not so surely prepare a young woman for successful journalism as a good working knowledge of forceful every-day English.

A less ambitious but not less honorable career is open to young women who choose to become the assistants of mothers in bringing up their children. I do not mean by this merely the nursery governess or the governess of older children. The mother assistant is more like an aunt or an elder sister as she fits into the household, and relieves the mother of burdens. We are learning that little children should not be given over into the hands of ignorant and illiterate peasant women from other lands, just in the period when they are most easily impressed by companionship with those about them. The office of mother's assistant should be filled by an educated lady, and no college graduate need hesitate to assume it. Also, there are women of large means who are able and willing to pay liberally for such service.

I hope there are a multitude of girls who, when college days are over, will be willing and happy to remain quietly at home, filling in the chinks there and blessing the lives of their parents. In our time, it is almost exceptional to find a grown-up daughter who is not reluctant to do this; each longs for a sphere of wider occupation. But to some the Lord may have assigned only the household with its blessed obscurity; only the little lowly place in the vineyard, under his own eye.

"One thing is needful." Still we hear him saying this, and if of any one of us he shall say that she hath "chosen the good part," what more can we desire? To be thorough, to be conscientious, to be diligent and faithful, are the needs of the hour for all women.

> From silken cords of earth's delight,
>   From iron chains of care,
> O set us free when in thy sight,
>   Dear Lord, we kneel in prayer.
>
> Forbid that dreams of ease and cheer,
>   Or transient thoughts of pride,
> Should make a chilling atmosphere
>   To drift us from thy side.
>
> Forgive if moaning discontent
>   In unbelief complains;
> Forgive if, when our hearts are rent,
>   We think but of their pains.
>
> Still come thyself in darkest hours
>   And cleave the gloom with rays
> So bright that all our grateful powers
>   Shall turn from grief to praise.

Trustful To-morrows

Still consecrate our joyful times
  With bliss beyond compare,
While faith the spirit's strength sublimes
  And robes of light we wear.

Oh, lift us to the better life!
  The shadows come and go,
But where thou art above the strife,
  The winds of heaven blow.